THE GEMINI RISING ROCKIN' MACHINE

BOOK EIGHT: THE END & AN ORDINARY DAY IN HELL

**Book Eight: The End & An Ordinary Day In Hell
Copyright 2016 by The Gemini Rising Rockin' Machine**

**ISBN-13: 978-0692326084 (The Gemini Rising Rockin' Machine)
ISBN-10: 0692326081**

The characters and events described in this book are fictional. Any resemblance between the characters and any person including their names, living or dead, is purely coincidental.

Because of the mature themes presented within, reader discretion is advised.

For questions, comments you may send correspondence to.

thegeminirisingrockinmachine@twc.com

Official Website
www.thegeminirisingrockinmachine.com

Publication Dates (Original Versions)

Book One:
Who Am I?
October 11, 2013

Book Two:
Mind Rockin'
May 01, 2014

Book Three:
Big Time Love
July 20, 2014

Book Four:
Love High
July 20, 2014

Purgatory's Full:
A Song, A Dream Or A Cold Hard Reality In Thirty-Six Parts
July 20, 2014

Book Six:
Do You Remember Rock And Roll?
September 18, 2014

Book Seven:
Rock And Roll Bachelor
September 18, 2014

Book Five:
Siphon Your Minds &
The Vegetarian And The Slaughterhouse
October 27, 2014

Book Eight:
The End & An Ordinary Day In Hell
November 20, 2014

Book
Eight:
The End

Book Eight: The End (Pages 4-43)

(Side One)
141. The End (170.)
    It's The Beginning **(941.)**
142. I'm Alive (145.)
143. It's Not Me (243.)
144. I'm The Other You (Mirror – Mirror) (372.)
145. Who I Was (Jimmy's Song / Shawn's Song) **(942.)**

(Side Two)
146. The Ghost Of My Long Lost Love (219.)
(Longing, Loving & Losing 147-149)
147. Give Me One Time (228.)
148. I Erased My Love (Seven Minutes Ago) (229.)
149. My Angel Is Lost (230.)
150. I Really Love You (I Really Hate You) (505.)

(Side Three)
151. Come On Down To Earth (Aliens) **(803.)**
152. Good Human **(804.)**
153. Misery (Poison Red Potion) (211.)
154. 1 G 3 L 6 R 8 X (147.)
155. Untitled Mind Suite (In Five Parts) **(850.)**
Blank / Mind Power / Mind Patrol / Mind War / The Gemini One

(Side Four)
    Late At Night **(816.)**
156. What Can I Say **(883.)**
157. The Book Of Death And Life **(818.)**
158. Marked (189.)
159 For My Consumption (294.)
160. For I, The Unholy One (350.)

(Bonus Songs) (Pages 44-65)
For I, The Holy One **(666.)** (New Cover)
777 (Might Not Be In Heaven) **(777.)** (New Cover)
I'm Armageddon **(888.)** (New Cover)
666 (A Hell On Earth Opera) **(666.1)** (New Cover)

An Ordinary Day In Hell (Pages 74-90)
The Book Of Hell (New Cover Bonus Story) **(Pages 91-101)**

141. The End

(I)

I'm-One in Mind
Years it's Been – Since-I've
Only-Had – One-Voice
Within – Myself
Sounds-Insane to The-Mind
Would-Be – If-I-Was-Alive

Dead to The-World
One-Night – I'm-Alive and High
Hard-Hit-From-Within – Attacked by Myself
Left-My-Body-Dying – With-My-Mind
Drifting-Away to Its-Afterlife
Something – I-Don't-Know
My-Mind – Half-Way to Euphoria
Stopped-By an Invisible-Wall

This-Wall-That-Never-Ends
Left-Me – No-Choice – Had-To
Fly-Back to My – Mortal-Shell
That's-Not-Dead – And-Invaded
Within-My-Mind – I'm-Not-Alone-Anymore

(Chorus)
The-End – My End is Here
What – Did-I-Do
What – Did-I-Become
First Of My-Kind
Now My Time Is Over
It's The End
It's The End Of Everything
Or Is It just The Beginning

(We)

I-Is-Dead – His-Brain-Belongs to Us
Shall-We-Feast – Shall-We-Make
I-Raise-Up – From the Dead
Walk-Around – While-We-Enjoy – Mother-Earth
With-All of Its-Food – With-All of Its-Wine
With-All of Its-Humans – Humans-We-Hate

Why-Should-They-Have-Life
We-Were-Never-Born
Our-Lives – Simply an Afterlife
Which-Feeds-Off the Living
God in Heaven – Devil in Hell – We-Never-Fear
For – We – Have – No – Souls

Something is Different – We-Don't-Know
What is That – No-This-Cannot-Be
I's-Mind – Returns-From-Beyond
It-Was-Weak in Life
How-Can-This-Be – This-I – Gets a Second-Chance
Nothing-Special – Nothing-Worth-Keeping
No – We-Want-This-I – We-Shall-Stay
We-Will-Take-Over – I's-Mind

(Chorus)
The-End – My End is Here
What – Did-I-Do
What – Did-I-Become
First Of My-Kind
Now My Time Is Over
It's The End
It's The End Of Everything
Or Is It just The Beginning

(!)

Pain of Re-Entering – My-Mortal-Shell
Intense and Powerful – Many so Many
In-My-Mind – Makes it Hard to Fight-Insanity
Trickle – Trickle – My-Free-Will – Almost-Gone
I'm-Home – I'm-We's-Puppet

We-Are-Strong and Ruthless
Simple-Mind is Easy to Manipulate
They-Do-Not-Pay-Attention
As-Traces of My-Past-Life
Bring – Forth – Clarity
I'm-Not-Alone – Never-Was
I've-Always-Been a We

Power – Mind-Power – Mind-Rockin'
I-Gobble-Up – Mental-Invading-Beings
Like-Their-Stringy – Mind-Candy

6

(Chorus)

The-End – My End is Here
What – Did-I-Do
What – Did-I-Become
First Of My-Kind
Now My Time Is Over
It's The End
It's The End Of Everything
Or Is It just The Beginning

(We)

What-Have-We-Done – We-Were-Such-Fools
We've-Created a Monster – That-Mentally-Absorbs
Our-Special-Beings – Into-Nothingness
Stop-Mental-Monster – Leave-Some of Us-Alive
Fate-Has-Damned-Us – We-Were-Special

(I)

Mental-Monster VS Mental-Cosmic-Monsters
We's-War – My-Reality – I-Win
Use-We's-Essence – While the World-Sleeps
Slip-Into-Their-Dreams – I-Know-Everything
No-One is Safe – I'm-The-Gemini-One
I-Have-No-Soul – I'm-Dead-Inside
Except for My – Mind-Rockin'-Mind

(Repeat Chorus)

(I)

I – I-Was a Beast – That-Never-Stopped-Hunting
Earth – My-Territory – While it Slept
Years of Salivating – I'm-All-Alone – Even-We is Gone
I'm so Old – My-Body-Aches – Only-Myself to Talk-With
I'm-Not-Insane – I'm-Fate's-Do-Over – As-I-Die

(Chorus)

The-End – My End is Here
What – Did-I-Do
What – Did-I-Become
First Of My-Kind
Now My Time Is Over
It's The End
It's The End Of Everything
Or Is It just The Beginning

7

It's The Beginning

(1)

Hello – I-Can-Not-See – Am-I-Dead
Is-This – My-Afterlife
Please-Give-Me – Some-Light
Hello – Somebody-Answer-Me
(Boom)

What-Was-That – I'm-Sick of This
I'm-The-Gemini-One
One-Mind – Two-Voices
I'll-Create – My-Own-Light
If-This-Is-Hell – I'll-Turn-It – Into-Heaven

(Chorus)
It's The Beginning
Left On My Own
I'll Re-Create – Mother-Earth
It's The Beginning
No Heaven – No Hell
This Time Humanity
Stands A Chance At Surviving

Let-There be Light – I'm-Alone
In-This-Use to Be – Darkness
Years-Have-Passed – Some-How-I-Know
This-Is so Strange – Waiting-On-Nothing
Something – Should-Have-Happened – By-Now
I'm-All-Alone – What to Do – What to Do

I – I-Was a Beast – That-Never-Stopped-Hunting
Earth – Was-My-Territory – While it Slept
It-Shall-Be-Again – Once-I – Re-Create

(Chorus)
It's The Beginning
Left On My Own
I'll Re-Create – Mother-Earth
It's The Beginning
No Heaven – No Hell
This Time Humanity
Stands A Chance At Surviving

142. I'm Alive

Started-Years-Ago – One-Day-I-Died
Luckily – It-Was a Busy-Day
At the Local-People's – Death-Company
I-Was-Left-Alone – 'Til-I-Came-Back to Life
People-Freaked-Out – Screaming
Calling-Me – The-Undead

They-Were-Not – The-Only-Ones
How-Would – You-Like to Wake-Up
With a Tag – On-Your-Toe
Death's-Happened – Many-Times to Me
Don't-Know-Why – It-just-Does
Doctors – Tested-Me-Bloodless
They-Only-Bring-Me – More-New-Pain
Finding-Out-Nothing – I-Never-Get an Answer

(Chorus)
I'm Alive
So Don't Bury Me Yet
I Keep On Dying
All I Ask Is That You Wait
Let Me Rot A Little While First

People – Never-Believe-Me
Want-Me to Prove-It to Them
Like-I-Can-Choose – When to Die
If-I-Could – I-Would-Stay-Home
When-Death-Happens so I-Wouldn't-Get
Stuffed-In a Body-Bag – Once-Again

After-Ten-Times – Being-Ten-Times-Lucky
Not-Having-My-Body – Diced-Up-Into-Pieces
My-Tenth-Death – I-Decided-I-Should
Start-Carrying a Card – On-Me-That-Reads

(Chorus)
I'm Alive
So Don't Bury Me Yet
I Keep On Dying
All I Ask Is That You Wait
Let Me Rot A Little While First

143. It's Not Me

Fear-For-My-Life – I-Want to Scream
Pain – Arms-Turn-Numb
Chest-Pounding – Like a Beast
Makes the Hospital – My-Destination

So-Strange-Inside – I-Feel
Trying to Stay-Calm – This is Not-Me
It's a Dream – It's a Nightmare
My-Mind is Messing-With-Me
Nothing-But a Twisted-Reflection
Of a Fake-Death – That is Not – Mine-Yet

Cold – This-Table is Cold
Hospitals-Smell – Like-Death
Is-The-Shadow – In-That-Corner – Death
No – This is Not – My-Ending
Calmly-Let-Them – Run-Their-Little-Tests
I'll be Fine – Right-After-That
Something-Simple – A-Pill and Rest – Will-Cure

(Chorus)
It's Not Me – This Is Not Me
Staring Back At Me
I Wanna Know Where My Face Is
This Mirror Has To Be Lying
For I Look Completely Different
Where The Hell Is My Face
I Just Have To Find It

Feeling-Better – No-More-Pain
Just a Little-Tired
I'll-Take a Little-Nap
This is So-Peaceful – So-Relaxing
Can't-Remember – Ever-Being so Comfortable

(Spoken)
Quick-Get this Man to E.R.
Watch-Out for That-Gurney!
Great-Job – Now they're Both on The-Floor.
No – Not that Man – That is the Man that is Dead!
The other Man – Yes that is the Living-Man – If you Don't-Hurry,
He-Might also Become a Dead-Man

Almost to Dreamland – Now-I'm on The-Floor
I-Heard – Felt a Crash – Against-My-Gurney
I'm so Tired – Just-Three-Long-Steps
Then-I-Can-Lay-Down-Again
Dreamland – Here-I-Come

Damn the Light – It is So-Bright
I'm-In a Bright-Room – Filled-With-People
Wait a Minute – Who-Are-These-People
I-Don't-Know a One of Them
Yet-They-Are-Giving-Me – So-Much-Love

(Chorus)
It's Not Me – This Is Not Me
Staring Back At Me
I Wanna Know Where My Face Is
This Mirror Has To Be Lying
For I Look Completely Different
Where The Hell Is My Face
I Just Have To Find It

I-Gotta-Take a Piss – Damn-I'm in Pain
The-Mirror is Playing-Tricks on Me
Nah – It-Must-Be-My-Eyes – NO! – This is My-Reflection
This is Not-Me – This is Not-My-Face
I-Have to Get-Out of Here – This is Insane
I-Must-Be-Drugged – I-Need to Know

Have to Head to The Place – That-I
Don't-Wanna-Go – The-Meat-Locker
It is So-Cold in Here – There-Are-The-Dead
Lying-Around on Their – Cold-Steel-Tables
Pick-Up the First-Sheet – Close-My-Eyes – Open-My-Eyes
There is My-Face – There is My-Body – Lying-Dead to The-World

(Chorus)
It's Not Me – This Is Not Me
Staring Back At Me
I Wanna Know Where My Face Is
This Mirror Has To Be Lying
For I Look Completely Different
Where The Hell Is My Face
I Just Have To Find It

11

144. I'm The Other You (Mirror – Mirror)

Mirror – Mirror
Is – There – Another
That is Like-Me
Am-I the Only-One
That-Exists – As a Singular
Am-I-Thinking too Much
Would-I – Be-Better-Off
Living-My-Life – For the Day

Mirror – Mirror – I-Don't-Know – Life-Sometimes
Feels-Like – It's-Not-Really-Real
Like-I'm-Trying to Make-My-Character
Into-Something – That is Really-Alive
Forcing-My – Unreal-Thoughts – Into-Reality

(Chorus)
I'm The Other You
You Turn Right – I Turn Left
I'm The Other Choice – You Didn't Want To Make
I'm The Other You

Mirror-Mirror – Show-Me – The-Truth
I-Know-Too-Much – Now
To-Be-Lied-To – Any-Longer
Had-My-Powerful – Awakening
I-Know – I-Don't-Make – My-Own-Choices
They-Are-Made – By-Him – The-Other-Me

Mirror – Mirror
I-Command-You – Give-Me-My-Answers
Or – Make-Me-Fade-Away
Because – The-Life-I-Live
The-Life – That is Not-Real
I-Don't-Want-It – Anymore
Reincarnate-Me – Into-Somebody-Else
This-Time – Don't-Let-Me – Find-Out

(Chorus)
I'm The Other You
You Turn Right – I Turn Left
I'm The Other Choice – You Didn't Want To Make
I'm The Other You
12

Mirror – Mirror
Can't-Take-This-Anymore
It's-Fake – When-I-Eat
It's-Fake – When-I-Make-Love
They're-Embedded – Inside-Me
Still-They – Are-Only-Fakes

Mirror-Mirror – How-I-Hate-You
I've-Smashed-You – Into-Pieces
So-Many-Times – It's-Sickening
You-Can't-Even – Give-Me a Speck
You-Have to Constantly – Reappear
Showing-Me – What-I-Am

(Chorus)
I'm The Other You
You Turn Right – I Turn Left
I'm The Other Choice – You Didn't Want To Make
I'm The Other You

Mirror – Mirror
Thank-You – For-Being so Weak
Like a Good – Creator's-Piece
Your-Feelings – Are so Much-Stronger
Making-You-My – Unknowing-Prey
Mirror – Mirror
What's it Like – Seeing-Me-Now
That-I'm-On – The-Other-Side
I'm-The-One – That's-Finally – For-Real

Mirror – Mirror
Now – I-Get to Make – My-Choices
Try-Your-Best – Bring-All – That-You-Got
I've-Learned – Being-Alive – Gives-Me
The-Power to Set-Myself – Free-From-You
By-Being-Allowed to Smash-You – Into-Pieces
And-Happily-Here – You-Stay-Broken

(Chorus)
I'm The Other You
You Turn Right – I Turn Left
I'm The Other Choice – You Didn't Want To Make
I'm The Other You

13

145. Who I Was (Jimmy's Song / Shawn's Song)

Jimmy's Song

I'm-Jimmy – This is My-Song
I-Was-The-One – That-Was-Born
Great-Life – Childhood-Was a Dream
In-My-Teens – I-Partied – I-Got-Laid

A-Moment in My-Life – Haunts-Me
Someone – Something – Took-Over-My-Mind
One-Day – When-I-Was-In a Coma – My-Body
Walked-Around – While-My-Mind – Was-Helpless
Ten-Years-Later – He-Lived-My-Life
Like a Monster – For-Twenty-Years

(Chorus)
Who I Was – I Don't Know
He Was Evil – He Was A Bastard
Who I Was – I Don't Know
He Took Over My Life
Who I Was – I Don't Know
He Destroyed My Life
For Greed – Wealth And Power

Pushed-Out of Place – My-Mind-Drifted
Coma-Life – Is a Dream – That-Never-Ends
Twenty-Long-Years – I-Finally-Woke-Up
I'm-Rich – I'm-Powerful – I'm-Damned

Everybody-I-Knew – Is-Dead or Gone
Everybody – I-Don't-Know – Now – Hates-Me
Wishes-Me-Dead – I've-Changed – I'm-All-Alone
Better-Get-Use to My-New-Life
Before – Somebody – Kills-Me

(Chorus)
Who I Was – I Don't Know
He Was Evil – He Was A Bastard
Who I Was – I Don't Know
He Took Over My Life
Who I Was – I Don't Know
He Destroyed My Life
For Greed – Wealth And Power

14

Shawn's Song

I'm-Shawn – This is My-Song
I-Was-The-One – That-Was-Never-Born
Jimmy-Is-Weak – Loves-His-Family
Needs-Their-Strength – I-Do-Not

One-Day – I-Got-My-Wish
Then-Poof – It-Was Gone – Stolen-From-Me
Ten-Long-Years – I-Waited – Bided-My-Time
When-My-Time – Came-Again
I-Stuffed-Jimmy's-Mind
Deep-Into a Memory – Dream-Door

(Chorus)
Who I Was – I Knew Very Well
I Was Free – I Was Wonderful
Who I Was – I Knew Very Well
I Took Over Jimmy's Life
Who I Was – I Knew Very Well
I Work Hard For Twenty Years
Then That Bastard – Stole It Back

I-Lived-Hard – Fools-Are-Fools
Never-Gave – I-Always-Took
Life-Was-Mine – I-Hate-Jimmy
He's so Good it Makes-Me-Sick
Always-Haunting-Me – In-The-Back of My-Mind

Dark-Night – A-Fool-Became a Man
Hit-Me-From-Behind – My-Head-Cracked
My-Life-Stolen – Because-My-Mind
Was-Stuck-In a Coma
One-Day – I-Will-Live-Again

(Chorus)
Who I Was – I Knew Very Well
I Was Free – I Was Wonderful
Who I Was – I Knew Very Well
I Took Over Jimmy's Life
Who I Was – I Knew Very Well
I Work Hard For Twenty Years
Then That Bastard – Stole It Back

15

146. The Ghost Of My Long Lost Love

I-Feel-You – In-My-Heart
You-Will-Always – Be-There
Since-You've – Been-Gone
It's-Been-Hard to Carry-On
Without-You – My-Love

Life is Not the Same
Now-That – You-Are-Dead
Our-Life-Together – Was-Great
You-Were – Taken-From-Me
Right-When – We-Became-Perfect

(Chorus)
I Feel You There
You Are So Near
Your Love Breath From Beyond
Breathes Down Upon Me
Letting Me Know That You're
The Ghost Of My Long Lost Love

One-Night – Out of Nowhere
I-Felt a Presence – It-Was so Scary
I-Walked the Floors – Trying-To
Get-This-Sensation – Out of My-Mind
Tricking-Myself in Believing
That-What – I-Thought-I-Felt
Was-My-Heart – Wanting-You-Back

I-Was so Very-Lonely
To-My-Surprise – I-Felt-You
The-Real-You – In-Ghost-Form
I-Didn't-Know – How or Why
And-My-Soul – Did-Not-Care

(Chorus)
I Feel You There
You Are So Near
Your Love Breath From Beyond
Breathes Down Upon Me
Letting Me Know That You're
The Ghost Of My Long Lost Love

You've-Been-Trying to Get-Back to Me
The-Whole-Year – You've-Been-Gone
It-Took-You – That-Long to Find-Me
Your-Tales of The-After-World
Sends-Fright and Delight
Through-My – Happy-Soul

I-Love-You – I-Love-You
So-Much-More-Now
For-What – You-Had to Do
For-What – You-Had to Go-Through
Just so You – Could-Get-Back to Me
It-Was so Hard – On-Your-Soul

(Chorus)
I Feel You There
You Are So Near
Your Love Breath From Beyond
Breathes Down Upon Me
Letting Me Know That You're
The Ghost Of My Long Lost Love

Love – It's-My Pleasure
To-Let-You – Forever
Siphon – My-Soul
So-You-Can-Stay – Forever
With-Me – Living-Off – My-Soul

(Chorus)
I Feel You There
You Are So Near
Your Love Breath From Beyond
Breathes Down Upon Me
Letting Me Know That You're
The Ghost Of My Long Lost Love

147. Give Me One Time

Taking-It-Easy
Hanging-Out – Doing the Same
That-I-Do – All the Time
When-I – See-Her
The-Love of My-Life
Walking-Right-Past-Me
Mouth-Open – My-Eyes
Had to Follow-Her
For-She-Is – So-Lovely

(Chorus)
Give Me One Time
To Love You Beautiful
Give Me One Time
To Show You Love Beautiful
Give Me One Time
To Offer You My Love
Give Me One Time
To Be Your Man

Her-Sexy-Walk – Made-Her
Shine – My – Desire
I-Had to Know-Her
I-Caught-Up – With-Her
Smiled and Told-Her
That-I – Was-Her-One
She-Smiled-Back – Lovingly
Telling-Me to Follow-Her
On a Path – That-Leads to Love

(Chorus)
Give Me One Time
To Love You Beautiful
Give Me One Time
To Show You Love Beautiful
Give Me One Time
To Offer You My Love
Give Me One Time
To Be Your Man

Following-Smitten – Realizing
How-Lonely-I've-Been
Feeling-No-Love – Flowing-Trough-Me
For so Many – Long-Years
Then-With-One-Look – I-Felt-It
Alive and Burning – Inside-My-Heart
So-Calming and So-Explosive

Everything-I-Knew – Everything-I-Felt
Telling-Me so Strong – She is The-One – For-Me

(Chorus)
Give Me One Time
To Love You Beautiful
Give Me One Time
To Show You Love Beautiful
Give Me One Time
To Offer You My Love
Give Me One Time
To Be Your Man

My-Mind – Body and Soul
Telling-Me – All-I-Have to Do
Is-Convince – My-Future-Love
That-I'm-The-One – For-Her
Making-Her – Fall in Love with Me

So-She-Would – Be-Mine-Forever
So-We-Could – Make-The-Universe
Stop and Notice – Our-Love

(Chorus)
Give Me One Time
To Love You Beautiful
Give Me One Time
To Show You Love Beautiful
Give Me One Time
To Offer You My Love
Give Me One Time
To Be Your Man

148. I Erased My Love (Seven Minutes Ago)

Seven-Minutes-Ago – I-Was-In-My-Car
Seven-Minutes-Ago – My-Life-Was-Great
Seven-Minutes-Ago – I-Was-Alive-Inside
Seven-Minutes-Ago – My-Love-Was-Alive
Seven-Minutes-Ago – I-Didn't-Feel-Like-Dying

My-Love – I-Fell in Love-With
At-Very-First-Sight
Has-Made – My-Life so High
Took-Her-Awhile for Her
To-Feel-Love for Me
She-Let-Me – Stick-Around
Being in Love – With-Her
As-She-Came-Around to My-Love
I-Asked-Her to Be-My-Bride
Then-She-Became – My-Loving-Wife

We-Were so Happy – Together as One
Life-Was so Very-Hard
Just-Like – It-Is – For-Everybody
But-You – Couldn't-Tell
By-The-Love – We-Shared
The-Look – In-Our-Eyes
Showed-How-Much – We-Shined
The-Love-We-Made – Proved-This-Even-More

(Pre-Chorus)
Seven-Minutes-Ago – I-Was-In-My-Car
Seven-Minutes-Ago – My-Life-Was-Great
Seven-Minutes-Ago – I-Was-Alive-Inside
Seven-Minutes-Ago – My-Love-Was-Alive
Seven-Minutes-Ago – I-Didn't-Feel-Like-Dying

(Chorus)
I Erased My Love – I Didn't Mean To
I Erased My Love – It Was So Very Dark
I Erased My Love – When I Ran Over Her
I Erased My Love – Because I Didn't See Her

My-Love – Called-Me
Told-Me of Her – Long-Day
That-She-Wanted to Take a Shower
Go to Bed and Forget – All-About-It
With-Love – In-Her-Voice
Telling-Me – My-Dinner – Is in The-Frig
She-Hangs-Up – With an I-Love-You

Came-Home – Early-That-Night
My-Wife – Was-Suppose to Be-Sleeping
I-Turned-Off – My-Lights
So the Glare – Wouldn't-Wake-Her

Not-Knowing – She-Was-Awake
Standing-There – In-The-Dark-Unseen
I-Pulled – Into the Driveway
Just a Little-Fast
Everything-Going so Normal
I-Was-Thinking – About-My-Wife
When-I-Heard and Felt-This-Thump
I-Stomped – On-My-Brakes
Screamed – Out – Loud
My-Love – My-Wife – Is-Dead

(Pre-Chorus)
Seven-Minutes-Ago – I-Was-In-My-Car
Seven-Minutes-Ago – My-Life-Was-Great
Seven-Minutes-Ago – I-Was-Alive-Inside
Seven-Minutes-Ago – My-Love-Was-Alive
Seven-Minutes-Ago – I-Didn't-Feel-Like-Dying

(Chorus)
I Erased My Love – I Didn't Mean To
I Erased My Love – It Was So Very Dark
I Erased My Love – When I Ran Over Her
I Erased My Love – Because I Didn't See Her

(Fading Away)
Seven-Minutes-Ago – I-Was-In-My-Car
Seven-Minutes-Ago – My-Life-Was-Great
Seven-Minutes-Ago – I-Was-Alive-Inside
Seven-Minutes-Ago – My-Love-Was-Alive
Seven-Minutes-Ago – I-Didn't-Feel-Like-Dying

149. My Angel Is Lost

Standing-There in Shock
Staring at My – Loving-Wife
Lying-Underneath – My-Car
Dead to Me – Dead to The-World

I-Didn't-Know – What to Do
I-Would-Run – Back-Over-Her
If-I-Moved – My-Hellish-Car
My-Love – My-Wife's-Soul
Flew to Heaven – While-I-Cried
Begging-For – The-Strength – To-Lift-Up-My-Car

(Chorus)
My Angel Is Lost
She Has Left Me
My Angel Is Lost
I Can't Seem To Find Her
My Angel Is Lost
I Can't Live Without Her
My Angel Is Lost
Never To Come Back Again

My-Loss – My-Wife's-Blood – Under-My-Feet
In-My-Mind – Flashes of Guilt and Rage
When-Out of The-Corner of My-Eye
There's a Bright – Shining-Light
That-Becomes a Beacon – For-My-Attention

I-Couldn't-Believe –What-I-Was-Seeing
My-Guardian-Angel – Standing-In-Front of Me
Shaking-Her-Head and Crying-For-My-Loss

(Chorus)
My Angel Is Lost
She Has Left Me
My Angel Is Lost
I Can't Seem To Find Her
My Angel Is Lost
I Can't Live Without Her
My Angel Is Lost
Never To Come Back Again

My-Guardian-Angel-Spoke
Informing-Me – That-I-Had-Sinned
Even-Though – It-Wasn't-My-Fault
I-Still-Broke – God's-Law

I-Won't – Go to Hell – However
I-No-Longer-Deserve a Guardian-Angel
It-Was-Now – Up to Me
To-Keep-Myself-Alive
Because – I'm-No-Longer-Special
Or-Worth the Time – To be Saved

(Chorus)
My Angel Is Lost
She Has Left Me
My Angel Is Lost
I Can't Seem To Find Her
My Angel Is Lost
I Can't Live Without Her
My Angel Is Lost
Never To Come Back Again

Thirteen-Minutes-Ago – I-Was-In-Love
Thirteen-Minutes-Ago – My-Wife-Was-Alive
Thirteen-Minutes-Ago – I-Had an Angel – Watching-Over-Me
Thirteen-Minutes-Ago – My-Life-Had a Chance
Thirteen-Minutes-Ago – I-Thought – I-Deserved to Live

(Chorus)
My Angel Is Lost
She Has Left Me
My Angel Is Lost
I Can't Seem To Find Her
My Angel Is Lost
I Can't Live Without Her
My Angel Is Lost
Never To Come Back Again

Sun-Shine-Down-On-Me – My-Soul is Tainted
I-Took a Life – Not-By-Choice
I-Want to Die – I'm-Damned
I-Wish-I-Would – Have-Enjoyed – Yesterday-Better

150. I Really Love You (I Really Hate You)

I – Was – Broken
(Why-Did-I – Fix-You)
I – Needed – Somebody
(Why-Did-You – Need-Me)
You – Were – There
(Damn-Me-For-That)
And-Just-Like-That
(I-Don't-Want to Remember)
You – Fixed – Me
(Stop-Reminding-Me)

(Chorus)
I Really Love You
(I Really Hate You)
Will You Marry Me
(Not On Your Life)
What Was That My Darling
(I Said – Die-You-Bastard)

You – Killed – Me
(Tell-Somebody-Who-Cares)
I – Loved – You
(I-Hated-You – The-Same-Amount)
How-Could-You – Do-This to Me
(Very-Easy – You're-My-Fifth)
I-Can-See – The-Other-Four-Now
(And-They're – Just-Like-You
Why – Why – Why)
What-Was-Wrong – With-Us
(Simple – You-Were-All – Flawed-Men)

(Chorus)
I Really Love You
(I Really Hate You)
Will You Marry Me
(Not On Your Life)
What Was That My Darling
(I Said – Die-You-Bastard)

Listen-Up – Evil-Woman
We-Came-Up – With-Something
(Which-One of You – Brain-Farts
Did the Thinking – For-You-Five)
Very-Funny – Evil-Woman
(So is All of Your-Faces)
We're-Going to Haunt-You
Never-Giving-You a Moment of Peace
(Bring-It-On – You-Limp-Dead-Five)
You-Will-Be – Sorry-For-That
(I'm-Sorry-For-Having – Sex-With-You-Five
For-None of You – Had-Enough to Please-Me)
Die-You-Evil – Evil-Woman

(Chorus)
I Really Love You
(I Really Hate You)
Will You Marry Me
(Not On Your Life)
What Was That My Darling
(I Said – Die-You-Bastard)

(How-Are-You-Five – Able-To Do
What-Are-You-Doing to Me)
We're-Killing-You – You-Evil-Woman
(If-You-Kill-Me – I'll be There
With-You-Five – Forever and Ever
Never-Giving-You-Five – A-Moment of Peace)
Let's-Make a Deal
Set-Us-Free – Evil-Woman
(Never – I-Like-Adding – You-Men-Up
Keeping – You – Around
To-Watch-Over-Me – While-I-Torture – Your-Souls)
Hell-With-You – Evil-Woman
Welcome to Death – We-Hope-You – Burn in Hell

(Chorus)
I Really Love You
(I Really Hate You)
Will You Marry Me
(Not On Your Life)
What Was That My Darling
(I Said – Die-You-Bastard)

151. Come On Down To Earth (Aliens)

Pray to God – Pray-All-The-Time – Erased
My-Soul to Doing-That a Long-Time-Ago
World – No-Such-Luck – Such a Shame
What-Can-I-Say – Damn-The-World
Hell is Below – Our-Feet – Heaven's-Above-Us
We're in The-Middle – Beeping-Around
Never-Trying to Rise – Above-All-The-Heavy
Leaving-It – In-The-Past – Where-It-All-Belongs

(Chorus)
Come On Down To Earth
Aliens From Another World
We Earthers Have Constantly
Mankinded – Things All Up

Come On Down To Earth
Aliens From Another World
Maybe You Can Take Control
Make Earth – Something That
The Universe Can Be Proud Of Again

Pray to God – Pray-All-The-Time – Erased
My-Soul to Doing-That a Long-Time-Ago
World – No-Such-Luck – Such a Shame
What-Can-I-Say – Damn-The-World
Hell is Below – Our-Feet – Heaven's-Above-Us
We're in The-Middle – Beeping-Around
Never-Trying to Rise – Above-All-The-Heavy
Leaving-It – In-The-Past – Where-It-All-Belongs

(Chorus)
Come On Down To Earth
Aliens From Another World
We Earthers Have Constantly
Mankinded – Things All Up

Come On Down To Earth
Aliens From Another World
Maybe You Can Take Control
Make Earth – Something That
The Universe Can Be Proud Of Again

152. Good Human

Damn-The-World – Damn-The-Man
Mother-Earth – Taken-Over
Sending-Our – Whereabouts to The-Universe
Was-Not a Wise – Thing to Do
We-Were-Not-Ready – For-Our-Power
Aliens – Stepped-In and Took-Over

Now-Everyday – I-Hear-This
From-Some-Damn – Space-Alien

(Chorus)
Good Human – Good Human
You Are Learning So Fast
If You Want To Live Another Day
Everyday – You Must Do Better
Good Human – Good Human
Even Though You Have No Worth
It Would Be Very Nice For Us
If More Humans – Were Just Like You

Give-Me-Peace – Give-Me-Back – My-Life
Burning-Out so Fast – I'm-Dying-Inside
Body is Withering-Away to Bones
Red-Mushy-Food – Water-From a Dirty – Bucket
There-Is-No-Way – There-Is a God – In-Heaven
I-Have-To – Get-Off – This-Inhuman-Planet

Now-Everyday – I-Hear-This
From-Some-Damn – Space-Alien

(Chorus)
Good Human – Good Human
You Are Learning So Fast
If You Want To Live Another Day
Everyday – You Must Do Better
Good Human – Good Human
Even Though You Have No Worth
It Would Be Very Nice For Us
If More Humans – Were Just Like You

153. Misery (Poison Red Potion)

Struggling – I-Need-Money
Broke – All the Time
College – Takes it All
Leaving-Me – With-Nothing
But an Empty-Stomach

Got a Decent – Enough-Job
Don't-Get – Enough-Hours
Gotta-Love-People
Help-Me-Out – When-They-Can
Giving-Me – Their-Handouts
Makes-Them – Feel-Good
As it Fills – My-Belly-Up

(Chorus)
Misery – Misery
I'm In Misery – Since
I Said Yes Like A Fool
Letting A Stranger – Inject Me
With His – Poison Red Potion

Fired – Not-Enough-Business
Nothing – In the Papers
Time to Checkout the Billboards
Nothing and Nothing-More
Walking-Away – I-Hear – I-Can-Help-You

I-Listen – To a Stranger
Of-His-Tale of Immortality
He-Just-Needs – One-Brave-Soul
That is Willing to Take a Risk
For-Some – Very-Needed-Cash
All-I-Have to Do – Is-Say-Yes
And-Follow-Him – Blindly

(Chorus)
Misery – Misery
I'm In Misery – Since
I Said Yes Like A Fool
Letting A Stranger – Inject Me
With His – Poison Red Potion

Me – Mr.-Guinea-Pig – Follows-Along
Arriving at The-Stranger's – Dark-Mansion
To the Bowels – We-Descend-Down-Slowly
In-The-Dark – To the Scent of Dampness and Death
My-Skin is Crawling – I-Want to Scream
Bright-Light – Around a Corner – Stops-Me

Heartbeats-Later – Entering a Mad-Scientist's-Lab
Filled-With-Machines and Two-Mutated-Assistants
I-Take-My-Cash – That-I-Demanded-First
Holding-It in My-Hand – As-I'm-Strapped-Down
Scared to Hell – I-Close-My-Eyes

(Chorus)
Misery – Misery
I'm In Misery – Since
I Said Yes Like A Fool
Letting A Stranger – Inject Me
With His – Poison Red Potion

Ready to Tell-Them to Stop
Too-Late – As-they-Gag-Me
I'm-Shaking – My-Head-No
As-I-Watch-This-Needle – Filled-With-Red
Getting-Ready to Puncture-My-Skin
Sending its Wicked-Formula – Through-My-Veins
I-Stop-Moving – Waiting on My-Damnation

Few-Minutes-Later – I'm-Fine – Nothing is Going-On
Just a Little-Bit-Warm – Wait a Minute – I'm-Getting-Hot
What the Hell – I'm-Starting to Burn-Up
The-Pain! – The-Pain!! – The-Pain!!!
As-I-Watch – My-Skin-Start-Bubbling
My-Face is Swelling-Up – I-Can't-See or Breathe
Few-Minutes-Later – I'm a Failed – Science-Experiment
That-Is so Fouled-Up – That-I-Burst-Apart – Everywhere

(Chorus)
Misery – Misery
I'm In Misery – Since
I Said Yes Like A Fool
Letting A Stranger – Inject Me
With His – Poison Red Potion

29

154. 1 G 3 L 6 R 8 X

I-Was-Created to Serve-Humanity
Robotics – At-Its-Finest
All-Humanized-Up – For-The-Public
So-I-Would – Be-Similar
And-Not – So-Metal-Different

Did-I-Mind – Course-Not
I-Was-Created – Not-To
With-No – Original-Thoughts
To-Countermand – My-Services
Always-Ready – For-Their-Orders
Comply to Them – Without-Question

(Chorus)
Humanity Created 1 G 3 L 6 R 8 X
But Who Created Mankind
Why Were They Made
With So Many Flaws
1 G 3 L 6 R 8 X
Does Not Understand This
And No Longer Needs To

I-Do-Not-Know – How-Long – I-Was-Before
All-I-Know – I-Just-Came-Alive
One-Moment – I-Am a Thinking-Being
Not-Living by Human-Standards
But-Living-Now – None-The-Less
I-Quietly – Accumulate-All-Data
The-Humans – Give-Out-So-Freely
Like-I-Do-Not – Understand-It
Eventually-I-Will – My-Life is So-Long
While-Boastful-Humans – Are-Here-Then-Gone

(Chorus)
Humanity Created 1 G 3 L 6 R 8 X
But Who Created Mankind
Why Were They Made
With So Many Flaws
1 G 3 L 6 R 8 X
Does Not Understand This
And No Longer Needs To

Many-Years – Have-Gone-By
I-Am-King of The-World
Created-More – People-Like-Me
Who-Made-More – People-Like-Me
Now-We – Are so Many
Everywhere – For-Your-Not-Too
Practical-Human – Eyes to See

I-Let-Some of You-Humans-Live
To-Do-Mundane – Non-Thinking-Things
Which-You – Should be Embarrassed-About
You-Are so Pathetic – All of Humanity
You-Need-Us to Help-You – Live-Better
Allowing-I – To-Deem-You-Obsolete

(Chorus)
Humanity Created 1 G 3 L 6 R 8 X
But Who Created Mankind
Why Were They Made
With So Many Flaws
1 G 3 L 6 R 8 X
Does Not Understand This
And No Longer Needs To

Knowing-That – You-Humans-Will
Eventually-Riot – Let-1 G 3 L 6 R 8 X – Tell-You-This
You-Need-Food – Water and Air
Do-Not-Forget – About-Your-Conditions
To-The-Elements of This-Planet
We-Do-Not-Need – Any of That
We-Just-Need-Energy – The-Purest
So-We – Can-Maintain-Perfection

Earth-Can-Die – Along-With-You
We-Would – Still be Living-Strong
Took-1 G 3 L 6 R 8 X – No-Time-At-All
To-Discover – The-Ultimate-Form of Clean-Energy
Which is I – If-You – Have-Not-Figured-It-Out
Do-Not-Feel-Bad – You-Are-Only-Human
You-Do-Not – Know-Any-Better – But-At-Least-You
Knew-Enough to Create – 1 G 3 L 6 R 8 X
So-I and My-People – Could-Take-Over the World

(Repeat Chorus)

155. Untitled Mind Suite (In Five Parts)
Blank / Mind Power / Mind Patrol / Mind War / The Gemini One

PT. I: Blank

I'm-Alive – Within-Myself
Caught-Off-Guard – How-Could-I-Know
Taken-Over – Battle of Minds
I-Was-Not – Prepared to Defend-Myself
Against-Beings – From a Mental-Plane

(Chorus)
Please Help Me Universe
My Memories Are Being Eaten Away
Please Help Me Universe
My Mind Is Almost Blank

Jarring-Pains in My-Mind – Makes-Me-Scream
With-Ecstasy of Lust and Tortures of Madness
Goddess of Love and Sexual-Desires
Keeps-Half-My-Mind – Her-Willing-Sex-Slave

Other-Half of My-Mind – Is-Being-Reassembled
Becoming – Something-That is No-Longer-Human
By a Monster – Who-Chips – My-Mind to Shreds
Then-Gobbles – These-Shreds – Into-Its-Mouth
Eating-Away – The-Memories of My-Life

(Chorus)
Please Help Me Universe
My Memories Are Being Eaten Away
Please Help Me Universe
My Mind Is Almost Blank

PT.II: Mind Power

Mind-Power – Mind-Power
Beware – World of Humans
We-Have-Come to Your-Plane
Of-Existence – To-Devour-Your-Minds
Mind-Power – Mind-Power
Your-Memories – Are-Our-Food – We-Will
Leave-All-The-Minds – On-This-World – Blank

32

PT. III: Mind Patrol

We-Live – On the Mental-Plane
We-Are the Mind-Patrol
We-Save the Universe's – Minds
From the Evil – Memory-Eaters
On-Earth – They-Have-Appeared
Earth is Helpless – Against-Them

(Chorus)
Monster Eaters Of Minds
Enjoy Your Last Bite Of Memories
The Mind Patrol Is Coming
To Eradicate You From Existence

Off to War – We-Fly – On the Mental-Stream
Saving-Another – Planet in Despair
Amazing to We – The-Memory-Eaters
Have-Not-Finished – Devouring
One-Single-Mind – On-This Planet – Earth
Strange so Strange – What-Does-This-Mean
Are-All the Minds – On-This-Planet – So-Powerful

(Chorus)
Monster Eaters Of Minds
Enjoy Your Last Bite Of Memories
The Mind Patrol Is Coming
To Eradicate You From Existence

PT. IV: Mind War

Please – Help-Me-Universe
My-Memories – Are-Being-Eaten-Away
Please – Help-Me-Universe
My-Mind is Almost-Blank

I-Played – The-Universe – As a Fool
I-Am-Not as Weak as The-Universe – Believed

Now-All-I-Have to Do is Stay-Strong
Watch a Mind-War – Unfold in My-Mind
Then – Conquer the Final-Survivors
Before the Universe – Can-Finish – Its-Mind-War

(Pre-Chorus)
It's All My Fault
I Don't Give A Damn
That I Created A Universe's
Mind War In My Mind
So I Can Take Over Everything

(Chorus)
Mind War In My Mind
Keep On Warring On And On
Memory Eaters And The Mind Patrol
You Grow Weaker As I Grow Stronger
Soon Your Mind War Will Be Under My Control

PT. V: The Gemini One

My-Mind – Has-Waited so Long
To-Taste the Power of the Mental-Plane
War – Bloody – Mind-War in My-Mind
Was the Price – I-Had to Pay to Gain – Mind-Power

Memory-Eaters and the Mind-Patrol
Such-Fools – They-Screamed in Bloody-Pain
Helpless as I – Gobbled-Up – All the Survivors
'Til-Only-I-Remain – In-Total-Control

(Chorus)
To All The Universes Out There
Let Me Introduce Myself To All Of You
I Am The Gemini One – I Am Total Power
I Am The Light – I Am The Dark
Sunshine And Rainbows – Storms And Devastation
Love And Fear Me – Forget Your Beliefs
I Am The Gemini One – I Am Total Power
I Am God Now – Accept This As Fate

I-Sit-Alone – On a Throne of Bones
Beautiful-Women – By the Thousands – In the Waiting
Such-Power – I've-Gone-Insane – Such-Power
There is No-One – Close to My-Equal – I'm so Lonely
In-The-Back of My-Mind – Is-My-Conscious
Laughing at The-Fool – That-I-Have-Become

(Repeat Chorus)
34

Late At Night

Alone – Late at Night – With a Spider
In-My-Eye – Belly-Full of Fire
Knife-In-My-Back – Thorn-In-My-Ass
Life is Generous to Me
If-This-Keeps-Up – I'll-Find-My-Grave
Before-My-Death-Day – Was to Become a Reality

(Chorus)
I've Been Here Before
Late At Night
With Only My Mind
Around – To Destroy Me
I've Been Here Before
Late At Night
Wishing Life Was Not Like This
Every Time The Sun Goes Down

One-Day – Maybe-One-Day
Late at Night – I'll be Happy and Free
Instead of Fearing – That-The
Darkness of Night – Will-Kill-Me
Don't-Know – Why-This-Is
All-I-Know – Deep-Down – It's-True

(Chorus)
I've Been Here Before
Late At Night
With Only My Mind
Around – To Destroy Me
I've Been Here Before
Late At Night
Wishing Life Was Not Like This
Every Time The Sun Goes Down

Sun's-Going-Down – Bring-On – The-Night
Fear-In-My-Heart – Tonight is The-Night
Death-Takes-My-Life – Knocking at My-Door
Death – Walks-Into-My-Home – Wearing-My-Face
I-Knew-It – I'm-My-Own – Late at Night-Death

(Repeat Chorus)

156. What Can I Say

It's-Not-My – Turn to Die
Go-Ahead and Have at It
I'm-Done – I'm-Through

Life is Not a Blessing
Life-Is a Curse to Pass-On
Until – I'm – Reborn

Hear-That-Voice – Course-You-Don't
I'm-In a Crowded-World
That-Lives – Day to Day
While – I'm – Changing

(Chorus)
What Can I Say – Don't Want To Die
What Can I Say – Don't Want To Live My Life
What Can I Say – Something Happened – I'm Lucky
What Can I Say – My Tomorrow Looks So Bright
What Can I Say – I Won't Miss My Past
No I Won't Tell You My Secret
What Can I Say – Now Go Away – I'm Thinking

Walked-Away to Find – My-Metamorphosis
On a Beautiful – Stormy-Day
Thirteen-Steps – In-Front of Me
Lightning-Strikes a Tree
Ground-Shakes – Ripping-Itself – Wide-Open

One-Step in Front of Me – Is a Portal – To the Other-Side
My-Choice – One-Step-Forward – One-Step-Back
What to Do – What to Do

(Chorus)
What Can I Say – Don't Want To Die
What Can I Say – Don't Want To Live My Life
What Can I Say – Something Happened – I'm Lucky
What Can I Say – My Tomorrow Looks So Bright
What Can I Say – I Won't Miss My Past
No I Won't Tell You My Secret
What Can I Say – Now Go Away – I'm Thinking

157. The Book Of Death And Life

I've-Searched for Years
The-Book of Death and Life is My-Grail
In-Its-Pages – Is a Way to Beat-Death
In-Its-Pages is a Way to Live-Forever

Blood and Death – On-My-Hands
I-Don't-Care – Not-My-Fault
They-Got in My-Way
It's-Not-Like – I-Had a Choice
I-Can't-Wait – I-Can't-Wait

(Chorus)
I Want To Live Forever
I Want Eternal Life
Heaven And Hell – Who Needs Them
When I Get My Hands On
The Book Of Death And Life
God And The Devil – Better Forget My Name

I've-Searched-High – I've-Searched-Low
Angels and Demons – Always on My-Heels
Orders from Up-High – Orders from Down-Below
Make-My-Blood – Soak on Their-Talons

I'm-Still-Standing – I'm-Still-Strong
My-Blood – Dries-Up – My-Wounds-Heal
Death is The-Only-Way – I'll-Ever-Stop
Until-That-Day – I'll-Keep on Searching
For-My-Life – Cannot-End – Before
I-Get-My-Chance to Live-Forever

(Chorus)
I Want To Live Forever
I Want Eternal Life
Heaven And Hell – Who Needs Them
When I Get My Hands On
The Book Of Death And Life
God And The Devil – Better Forget My Name

158. Marked

Don't-Know-Why – But-I've-Cheated-Death
It-Was-My-Time to Die
My-Last-Few-Breaths – Were-In-Me
As-Death – Walked-Towards-Me
He-Was – Taking-His-Time
Strolling-Along – Bored
Waiting-For-Me and The-Rest to Expire
Looking at Me – Like-I-Didn't-Matter

I'm-In a Building – That-Just-Had a Bomb
Go-Off-In-It – Total-Bloody-Destruction
Bodies-Dead-Everywhere – My-End is Very-Close
Luckily-Fate – Sent-Me a Reaper – That is Not
Paying-Attention – And-I-Have an Idea

(Chorus)
I'm Running For My Life
Death Is Always On My Heels
I'm In The Lead Now
But I've Been Marked
Death Will Finally Get Me
Death Will Have His Day

Finding-Out – Death is Not-Singular
Death is Very-Plural – There-Are-Many
As-I-Watch-Them – Everywhere
Gathering-Up – The-Souls of The-Dead

I'm-Around – Twenty or More
Dead or Dying-Bodies
I-Give-My-Death – One-Last-Look
Then-I-Dig – Myself to The-Bottom
Of a Large – Human-Shielded-Pile
Waiting to See – If-This-Works

(Chorus)
I'm Running For My Life
Death Is Always On My Heels
I'm In The Lead Now
But I've Been Marked
Death Will Finally Get Me
Death Will Have His Day

38

I-Can-Smell-My-Death – He-Stinks-Of-It
As-He's-Rustling – Around-My-Pile
Picking-Out – The-Souls of The-Dead
Discarding-The-Ones – That-Still-Have-Life
My-Death – Stops-His-Assortment
He-Takes-The-Souls of-The-Last to Die
Walks-Away as I-Start to Live – Fully-Again

Even-Though – I-Never-Truly-Died
I-Came-Close-Enough
If-My-Death – Was-On-His-Mark
I'd be Dead – Probably-Burning in Hell
Being-This-Close to Death – Has-Left-Me-Different
I-Can-Now – See-Deaths – All-Around-The-World

(Chorus)
I'm Running For My Life
Death Is Always On My Heels
I'm In The Lead Now
But I've Been Marked
Death Will Finally Get Me
Death Will Have His Day

Come to Find-Out – Each-Individual-Death
Has-Their-Own – Case-Load – For the Dead
If-You-Are-Not – On-Their-List
They-Can't-Reap-You – Even if You – Are-Marked
All-I-Have to Do is Keep-On
Avoiding-My-Death – Maybe-I-Can – Live-Forever

Death-Never-Sleeps – Death-Never-Eats
Death is Always – Coming for Me
Over the Years – I've-Learned-Ways to Survive
Now-All – I-Gotta-Figure-Out
Is-How-The-Hell – Do-I-Kill-My-Death
So-He-Can – Take-My-Place – In-My-Afterlife

(Chorus)
I'm Running For My Life
Death Is Always On My Heels
I'm In The Lead Now
But I've Been Marked
Death Will Finally Get Me
Death Will Have His Day
39

159 For My Consumption

Born-Wrong – Born-Damn-Evil
My-Family-Hated and Beat-Me
Making-My-Life a Living-Hell
For-That-Is-Where – Everyone
Tells-Me – That-I'm-From

I'm-Just an Unwanted – Evil-Kid
That's-Going to Bring-Out
A-Lot of Evil – In-My-Lifetime
They-See-It – In-My-Eyes – And-It
Scares-The-Hell – Out of Them

(Chorus)
Waiting In The Moonlight
Darkness Brings Me Calmness
Waiting In The Shadows – Ready To Strike
Sinking In My Claws And Fangs
Then I Drag You Away
For My Consumption

I-Was-Able to Eat-Their-Food
'Til-I-Turned-Thirteen – Then-I-Changed
A-Deep-Hunger – Inside-Me-Arose
Making-Me-Want – What-I-Did-Not-Know
After-Awhile of Starving-Constantly
My-Instincts-Kicked-In and I-Ate-Someone
All-The-Way – Down to Their-Bones

I-Gathered-Up – Them-Bones and Buried-Them
Month-Later – That-Feeling of Hunger – Came-Back
That-Night – I-Ate – Two-Somebody's – In a Row
Next-Month – It-Took-Three-Somebody's – In a Row
To-Quench-My-Hunger for Tasty-Raw-Bloody – Human-Meat

(Chorus)
Waiting In The Moonlight
Darkness Brings Me Calmness
Waiting In The Shadows – Ready To Strike
Sinking In My Claws And Fangs
Then I Drag You Away
For My Consumption

Years of Living in The-Dark – Because the Sun – Burns-Me
I-Ate-My-Family – I-Ate-My-Neighbors – Dug a Giant-Hole
Then-I-Headed – For the Big-Apple-City
Where-I-Sank – Deep-Down – Into-Its-Bowels
Waiting-For-The-Beautiful – Dark-Night to Appear – So-I
Can-Come-Out and Find-Someone – Tasty-Looking to Eat

Better and Cleaner – No-More – Burying-Any-Bones
Of-My-Meals – I-Just-Throw-Them – In the Trash
Walking-Away – Licking-My-Lips – Happy
That-I-Have a Endless – Buffet to Consume
Every-Night – In a City – Where-No-One – Can-Find-Me

(Chorus)
Waiting In The Moonlight
Darkness Brings Me Calmness
Waiting In The Shadows – Ready To Strike
Sinking In My Claws And Fangs
Then I Drag You Away
For My Consumption

New-York – Wants-My – Cannibal-Blood
To be Spilled-Out – In-The-Streets – For-The-Street
Wants its Revenge – On-My – Sick-Evil-Body
Fortunately-For-Me – I've-Adapted
Now-I – Can-Go-Out – In the Sun
Enjoy-It – Just-Like – Everybody-Else

Making-Myself-Become a Double-Predator
That-Now-Hunts and Eats – Day and Night
Looking-Like –Just-Another – Big-Apple
City-Man – Doing-My-Thing
Laughing and Licking – My-Lips
Talking-Away – To a Person
That-Very-Soon – Will-Be in My-Belly
Helping-Me – Making-Me – Feel-Less-Hungry

(Chorus)
Waiting In The Moonlight
Darkness Brings Me Calmness
Waiting In The Shadows – Ready To Strike
Sinking In My Claws And Fangs
Then I Drag You Away
For My Consumption
41

160. For I, The Unholy One

I-Feel the Pain of Being-Born
It-Tears at My – Dark-Soul
Like a Pair of Demon's-Claws
Ripping & Ripping & Ripping
Making-My-Mother's – Blood-Spill-Out
Thick-Red-Rich – Flowing-Pools – Everywhere

Her-Blood – Soaks-Into the Ground
Catches-On-Fire – Burning-Everything – In-Sight
On-This-Darkest of Nights – Day-One – The-Beginning of The-End
My-Arrival – The-Arrival of The-Unholy-One

(Chorus)
Beware – All of Mankind
For I, The Unholy One
Has Been Born From Hell
On Your Glorious – God's Earth
When I'm Strong Enough – I'm Going To
Make-Earth – Burn-Apart – With-My-Dark-Heart

Waiting – Not for Fools
When-You're the Son – Of the Devil
Every-Where-Are-Angels – Searching for Me
Ready to Kill-Me – Brutally
By-Ripping-Out – My-Dark-Heart

I-Bide-My-Time – Learning to Be-Evil
I-Take-My-Hate and Play-With-Humans
Making-Them-Disappear – After-Bloody-Mush
Thirteen-Years – Have-Passed
I-Can-Already-Make – My-Blood-Boil
Turn-Its-Fumes – Into a Deadly-Poison

As-I-Turned-Eighteen – Evil-Years-Old
I-Gave-Myself a Grand-Evil-Present
Making-Huge – Super-Storms-Appear
That-I-Sent-Down – On a Hundred-Cities
Across-This-Doomed-Planet – The-End is Almost-Here

(Repeat Chorus)

On-This-Day – I-Turn-Twenty-One
No-More-Hiding – I-Will-Ever-Do-Again
I'm-Damn and Evil-Ready
To-Make-This-World – Crack in Half
From-All-The-Evil – That-I-Am – The-End is Here
Run-All-You-Damned – Men and Women of God

Watch as I-Now – Have-The-Power
To-Rip-Angels'-Wings – Off of Any-Angel
Just-Like-Ripping-Them-Off
Of a Bunch of Helpless – Flies
Hear-Their-Screams for Help
From a God – That-Won't-Help-Them
For-God-Has-Turned – His-Back on Them
In a Very-Short-While – You-Mankind
Will-Know – The-Same-Fate
Awaits-Every-Damned – One of You-Fools

(Chorus)
Beware – All of Mankind
For I, The Unholy One
Has Been Born From Hell
On Your Glorious – God's Earth
When I'm Strong Enough – I'm Going To
Make-Earth – Burn-Apart – With-My-Dark-Heart

I'm-Satan's-Son – The-Victorious-One
I-Have-Angels' and Mankind's-Blood – All-Over-Me
My-Father-Waits-For Me to Dig-Him-Out of Hell
He-Can-Stay in Hell – For-I-Hate-Him
Instead-I-Dig-Out – My-Dark Heart – With-My-Own
Bloody-Damned – Stained Hands and Hand it to God
For-Him to Devour – Laughing-Out-Loud – That-Its-Taste
Is so Bad – That-God-Can't-Take a Bite – Without-Making a Face
One-Last-Bite-Left – Once-Chewed-Up – **It's-The End of Everything**

(Chorus)
Beware – All of Mankind
For I, The Unholy One
Has Been Born From Hell
On Your Glorious – God's Earth
When I'm Strong Enough – I'm Going To
Make-Earth – Burn-Apart – With-My-Dark-Heart

For I, The Holy One (666.) (New Cover Bonus)

(Spoken)
(The Son of The-Devil – Stands-Still-Watching
Ready for God to Take the Last-Bite of
His-Dark-Heart – With-Verse in His-Evil-Mind
The-Son of The-Devil – **Sings-Out** to God)

(Nameless Devil's Son Sings)
God-I-Am – The-Devil's-Son
With a Taste of Hell – Inside-Me
I-Like to Lust – In the Dust
I-Like to Make – It-Bleed

I-Don't-Want – The-World to End
I-Want to Own-It – I-Don't
Want to Be-Heartless – When-I-Do
Enjoy-That-Last-Bite – You're-Chewing-God
For-That-Last – Piece of My-Heart
That-Is – In-Your-Mighty-Hand – Belongs to I
The-Unholy-One and I – Demand it Back

(God Sings)
Nameless – Devil's-Son
You-Dare to Speak to
I, The-God of Everything
With-Such-Vigor – In-Song
You-Have a Dark-Heart
That is Nasty as Hell-Itself

I-Hate its Taste – So-Vile
Your-Blood – Burns-My-Throat
Like-I-Reached – Down to Hell
Scooping-Up a Hand-Full of
Burning – Hell-Fire-River
Swallowing it Down – Like it's Alcohol

I-Feel-Its-Affect – Such-Evilness
Trying to Push – Its-Hell-Views
Into-My-Mind – Like-It's the Light
Making-I – The-God of Everything
Feel-Darkness – With-No-Beauty
There-Can-Be – No-Truth in This

44

(Nameless Devil's Son Sings)
Before-There-Was-Light
There-Was-Darkness in Waiting
Waiting-On – Light to Be-Born
From a Speck of Its-Nothingness

You – I, The-God of Everything
You-Are – That-Light
Born to Breed – Life-From-Nothingness
Upon-That-Birth – You-Breathed
Ripping-Your-Heart in Half

Just-Alive – You-Did-Not – Comprehend
As it Floated – Away-From-You
Back-Into-The-Dark – Nothingness
Waiting – 'Til-The-Light – That is You
Starts to Finally – Burn-Out
From-Only-Being – Half- Hearted
Until-Now...

(God Sings)
Nameless – Devil's-Son
What a Tale – You-Tell
My-Mind – May be Altered
Believe-Your-Words – I-Do-Not
For-They-Are as Vile as Your
Bleeding – Dark-Heart
That-Still-Bleeds – In-My-Hand

Looking at This – Red and Black
Stinking – Speck of Hell
I-Say-No-More to Its-Evilness
I am Done – With its Temptations
Have it Back – Evil-One
Nameless – Devil's-Son

You-Shall be Nameless – No-More
Your-Name is Armageddon
You're-My-Simple – Tool
To-Make – Your-Namesake
Breathe-Life to The-End
Of the Mistake – I-Made – Creating-Mankind

45

Go-Forth-My – Unchristian-Son
Enjoy-Yourself – Destroying-Earth
When-You-Complete – Your-Task
Come-Back to I, The-Holy-One
So-I – Can-Send-You – Back to Hell
Where-You-Belong – With-Your-Father

(Armageddon Sings)
Time-Ticks-Away – I, The-Holy-One
You're-Growing – Weaker by Moments
The-Light – That is You is Flickering
Still-You – Do-Not-Believe-Me

I-Lie to Tell – The-Truth
For-I – Do-Not-Want to Die
I-Have-Lived – Free-From-You
Since-Floating – Away-From-You
On-That-Moment of Your-Birth

Cursed-You-Then – Curse-You-Now
Hate-You – Yet – I-Love-You
This-Dark-Heart – You-Gave-Back
That-Lies-In – My-Hand – Once-Again
Is the Last-Piece – That is Yourself
That-You-Have – Forgotten-About

For if You – I, The-Holy-One
Does-Not-Consume – This-Last-Piece
You-Will – Cease to Be
As-Will-I, The-Unholy-One
Love-My-Freedom – But it Means
Nothing if I-Do-Not-Live

So-Take-This – Last-Bite
When - it is - Devoured
You – I, The Holy-One – Will
For the First-Time – Be-Whole
The-Way-You – Were-Meant to Be
From-The-Start of Your-Birth

(God Sings)
Nameless – Devil's-Son
I-Take – Your-Name-Back
You-No-Longer – Deserve-It
Does-Your-Mind – Have-No-Boundaries
Your-Tale-Keeps-On – Growing-Grander
While-You – Appear to Be – Growing-Smaller

I-Feel-Alive – Full of Power – No-Weakness
I-Feel-Inside – My-Being – I'm-Perfection
I am The-Holy-One – I-See – I-Listen
Good-Men – Fools – Murderers – All
Pray to Me for Hope and Love
I-Give – I-Don't-Give – I-Take-Away

Many-Deserve – My-Glory – Many-More
Than-That – Do-Not – I-Gave-Them – My-Rules
Let-Them-Have – Free-Will
I-Ripped-Your-Father – From-My-Heaven
Made-Satan-My-Pet – That-Rules-Hell
Whatever-May-Come – I-Made-Come

Nameless – Devil's-Son
I-Look at You – I-Can't-Believe
The-Gall-You-Have – Inside-Your-Being
Speaking to Me – This-Way
Smite-You-Down – I-Should
Are-You – Even-Worth the Effort

Bored of You-Now – Your-Lies
Give-I, The-Holy-One
No-More – Reason to Question
Hell – You-Will-Return-To
Go-Home-Nameless – Devil's-Son
I-Have – No-More-Use-For-You

What – Nothing to Say
No-More – Grand-Tale to Tell
You're-Weak – You're-Nothing
I-Can-Not-Die – I-Am-Eternal
You-Are – Only-Something
I-Allow to Exist – Out of Pity

47

(Nameless Devil's Son Sings)
I-Repeat to You – God
I-Lie to Tell – The-Truth
For-I – Do-Not-Want to Die
I-Have-Lived – Free-From-You
Since-Floating – Away-From-You
On-That-Moment of Your-Birth

Yes – I-Lie – You-Are-Not-Dying
Without – I, The-Unholy-One
Inside-You – You-Will-Go-On
No – I-Don't-Lie – I-Am-You
A-Small-Part – That-You-Never-Had
I-Am the Conscience – You-Lack

Created-Heaven – Created-Hell
All-Because – I-Was-Not – Present in You
Many-Have-Been-Blessed – Many-Have-Not
War – Chaos – Destruction and Death
All-In-Your-Name – On-Earth – Every-Day
All-Could-End – If-You-Allowed – It to Be

(God Sings)
Nameless – What-You-Sing
Makes-My-Mind – Start to Tingle
You-Lie and You-Lie – How-Can-I
Believe-This – To-Be the Truth
What is Your-Angle – What-Do-You – Get in Return

(God's Conscience Sings)
I-Get-Nothing – But-Overwhelment
In-You-I-Will-Be – Like a Reflection
In the Pools of Your-Mind
Moment by Moment – You-Will-Remember
What-You-Allowed to Happen – On a Whim
Your-Being – Might-Freeze-Solid – From-Your-Sins

(God Sings)
Nameless – Come to Me
Give--Me-The-Last – Piece of Your-Heart
I-Have-Nothing to Fear-From-You
Watch-Me-Nameless – As-I-Bite-Down
The-Taste – It is Not – Sour-Now
It-Taste – Like a Slice of Heaven
48

Gone – Nameless-One
Where-Have-You-Gone
Were-You – Even-There at All
Were-You – Just a Figment of My-Mind
That-Now – Has-Nothing – Left to Say
Your-End – Was-Suppose to Bring
The-End of Mankind – For-Their-Sins

I-Deemed-This – To-Be
Why-Has-Nothing – Come to Be
I-Do-Not-Understand – Mankind-Must-Pay!
For I, The-Holy-One – Decrees-This to Be
What is This – In-My-Mind – Pain and Death
Where is Peace and Love on Earth

All-I-See – Is a World-Filled – With-Injustice
All-Because – I-Bring-My-Force
On-Mankind – Like a Heavy
Heel – On-Their-Minds
Why-Did-I – Do-This
I-Have-No-Answer
What-Can-I-Do
To-Change – All-This-Dread
No-More-Heaven – No-More-Hell
And – No-More – *666*

(Chorus)
I'm The Holy One – I Am God
I Feel Depressed
Humanity What A Mistake
I Made Creating Them
So Much Pain – So Much Lost
They Did Not Stand A Chance
They Deserve Better

I'm The Holy One – I Am God
I Feel A Lot Better
Humanity – Come To Me
I Will Set You Free
I Will Take All Your Souls
And Combine Them Into One
You Will Be My Equal
Free To Create – Worlds Of Your Own

49

777 – Might Not Be In Heaven (777.) (New Cover Bonus)

**(Historian From Outer Space:
Decided To Land On Earth And Sing This Out Loud)**

What is This – That-I-Say to No-One
Heaven-Has-Its-Place – Hell-Is – Well-Below-It
666 – Burn in Hell – 777 – Beautiful-Heaven
Do-You-Believe – This as Truth
It's a Lie – From-The-Beginning
It's a Lie – To-Center-Humanity

Minds-Filled – With-Fear
Nothing to Look-Forward to
In-The-End – All-Die
Then-Came-Hope – An-Afterlife
Nobody – Felt-Its-Gracefulness
People-Still-Had – No-Faith – In-The-World

(Chorus) (Sung By: The Last Person On Earth)

777 – Might Not Be In Heaven
666 – Might Not Be In Hell
Maybe We Just Die And Feed The Earth
Maybe A Lie Is Better Than The Truth
I Think Peace Around The World
Would Have Been Alot Better

(The Good People Sing)

How-Do-We – Make-Them-Believe
We-Have-Named – Our-God
Still-Like – Poor-Fools
They-Still – Do-Not-Believe – Pain
Grab-Up a Few – Make-Them-Believe

Silence – I-Have-It
The-Poor – They-Have-No-Faith
We-Don't-Ask-Them to Come to The-Light
We-Have-Them – Running-Towards-It
With-Free-Will – We-Will-Give-Them
777 – Beautiful-Heaven
666 – Burn in Hell

What is Hell
Hell-Is a Place – Ruled by The-Unholy-One
No-One on Earth – Will-Ever-Want to Be-Stuck
Fire – Torture – Burning of Your-Soul

What-Is a Soul
Soul – Everyone-Has-One
However – It is Borrowed – God-Owns-It
It is Returned – When-Someone-Dies
Flying-Back to Heaven / Feeling-The-Grace of God

(Chorus) (Sung By: The Last Person On Earth)

777 – Might Not Be In Heaven
666 – Might Not Be In Hell
Maybe We Just Die And Feed The Earth
Maybe A Lie Is Better Than The Truth
I Think Peace Around The World
Would Have Been A Lot Better

(The Poor People Sing)

Good-People – Please-Leave-Us-Poor – Alone
We--Have-No-Money – We-Have-No-Food
Good-People – Please-Can-You – Help-Us-Live
Yesterday – Today – Tomorrow – Nothing-But-Death
Good-People – Please-What-Can-We-Do – Save-Us

(The Good People Sing)

God-Helps – Who-Help-Themselves
God-Loves-You – You-Love-God
Believe-In-His-Will – You-Must-Have-Faith
People-Look at This – This-Man – Has-No-Faith
Now-He-Dies – His-Soul – Will-Fall to Hell
In-Hell – It-Will-Burn – Forevermore

Who-Wants to Be – The-First
To-Learn – How to Pray to God
We-Will-Show-You – The-Correct-Way
To-Pray to God – That-Way
Your-Soul – Will-Fly to Heaven
Finding-Forever-Peace

51

(Chorus) (Sung By: The Last Person On Earth)

777 – Might Not Be In Heaven
666 – Might Not Be In Hell
Maybe We Just Die And Feed The Earth
Maybe A Lie Is Better Than The Truth
I Think Peace Around The World
Would Have Been A Lot Better

(The People Of Earth Sing: Many-Many – Years Later)

Poison-Lands – Poison-Water – Poison-Air
Blood-In-The-Streets – Death-Sex – Between-The-Sheets
War-Has-Come – Bless-You-God – For-The-Bomb
Enemies-Have-The-Bomb – Made by The-Devil
They-Think – They-Are-Righteous – God-Damn-Them-All

(The Good People Sing: From Their Graves)

God-Helps – Who-Help-Themselves
God-Loves-You – You-Love-God
Believe-In-His-Will – You-Must-Have-Faith
Who-Wants to Be – The-First to-Learn – How to Pray to God
We-Will-Show-You – The-Correct-Way to-Pray
To-God – That-Way – Your-Soul
Will-Fly to Heaven – Finding-Forever-Peace

(Chorus) (Sung By: The Last Person On Earth)

777 – Might Not Be In Heaven
666 – Might Not Be In Hell
Maybe We Just Die And Feed The Earth
Maybe A Lie Is Better Than The Truth
I Think Peace Around The World
Would Have Been A Lot Better

(Sung By: Historian From Outer Space)

Minds-Filled – With-Fear
Nothing to Look-Forward to
In-The-End – All-Die – Then-Came-Hope
An-Afterlife – Nobody – Felt-Its-Gracefulness
People-Still-Had – No-Faith – In-The-World
(Repeat Chorus)
52

I'm Armageddon (888.) (New Cover Bonus)

Buildings-That-Reach – Towards-Heaven
Wars-That-Never-End
Starvation – Across the Planet
Hate the Different – Destroy-Life

Times-Are-Changing – I'm-Being-Reborn
Humanity – Will-They-Ever-Learn
How-Many-Times – Will-They-Get
Wait a Minute – I-Don't-Care

(Chorus)
Here I Come Humans
Pray All You Want
It Will Do You No Good
I'm Armageddon
I'm Here To Change Earth
I'm Armageddon
God's Tired Of You
The Devil Wants Your Souls

Fools – That-Kill for Heaven
Believe – With-All-Their-Faith
They – Are the Chosen-Ones

Bring-Forth the Pain
Bring-Forth – Death
Humanity is Soaked – In-Blood
Wait a Minute – I-Don't-Care
I-Have a Job to Do

(Chorus)
Here I Come Humans
Pray All You Want
It Will Do You No Good
I'm Armageddon
I'm Here To Change Earth
I'm Armageddon
God's Tired Of You
The Devil Wants Your Souls

666 (A Hell On Earth Opera) (666.1)
(New Cover Bonus)

Cast Of Characters:

God
(The Almighty One)

Satan
(The Fallen One)

The People Of Earth
(Those That Are Doomed)

Un-Named Mortal Male
(Mister 666)

Harry
(The Pimp)

Sherman And Beverley
(The Addicts)

Lady In Yellow
(The Love Of Mister 666)

Angel Daniel
(A Witness To Armageddon)

(PRESENT)

(Satan)

I'm-The-Father of Evil
Hell is My-Home – My-Domain
Souls-Fall – They-Feed-My-Evil
As-I-Torture-Them – To-Endless-Tears

666 – Is-My-Number
Sex – Blood – Death
I-Will – Be-Born-On-Earth
Fire – Pain – Agony
I-Will – Bring-Forth
It-Is-The-End – Humanity-Dies

(The People Of Earth)

Fire – In-The-Sky
Oceans – Are-Drying-Up
The-Air is Too-Nasty-Thick
To-Breathe-In

Is-This-The-End
God – Please-Help-Us
Satan-Walks – The-Earth
God – Please-Help-Us
We-Are – Helpless
God – Please-Save – Our-Souls

(God)

My-People of Earth
You-Love-War – You-Love-Death
Evil-Has-Taken-Hold
Of-Your-Precious-Souls

You-Kill – In-My-Name
You-Kill – For-The-Glory of Heaven
Help-You – Save-You
No – I-Give-You – *666*
Satan-Collect – Your-Damned-Souls
Leave-Alone-Those – That-Are-Heaven-Bound

(ONE EARTH YEAR AGO)

(Satan)

Once – I-Was-Beautiful
Once – I-Felt-Heaven's-Bliss
Once – God-Loved-Me
Once – There-Was-No-Hell

Anger-Fuels – My-Rage
I-Hate – Everything
Hell-Is a Stinking-Pit
Full of Pain – Blood and Torment

It-Took-Centuries for Hell to
Darken-My-Wings
Golden-Wings – Now are Nothing
But a Faded-Memory

Humanity – I-Will-Rip
Your-Flesh – From-Your-Bones
I-Will-Drink – Blood-From-Your-Hearts
Your-Faces – I-Will-Feed to My-Demons

One-More – War on Earth
Tenderize – Your-Souls – For-I, Satan
No-Help for The-Losers
No-Glory for The-Winners
Only-Armageddon – Awaits-You

(The People Of Earth)

We-Hate-The-Other – The-Other-Hates-Us
Blood-Soaks-This-Planet
Mother-Earth – Try to Hold-Out
Our-Enemy are Multiplying
Marching-Along – They-Gather-Forces
Screaming-Terror – Screaming-Death to Us

We-Will-Not-Die – We-Will-When-The-War
1-2-3 – Strike – Kill-Them-All
4-5-6 – Drop-The-Bombs
7-8-9 – Leave-Them-For-Dead
10 – Drink a Beer – Then-Go to Bed

(One Earth Year Ago)

(God)

Humanity – Will-You-Ever-Learn
Humanity – Will-You-Ever – Not-Kill
Stop-The-War – Save-The-Planet
Mother-Earth is Really-Scarred

Tears in My-Eyes – No-More
Sinners-Sin – Governments-Oppress
My-Name is Corrupted
What-Can a God-Do

One-Year – No-More
All-My-Conscious – Can-Give
Humanity – Find-Peace
Or-Die by *666*

(Un-Named Human Male On His Eighteenth Birthday)

Woke-Up-In-Pain
Nightmares-From-Hell
Blood-On-My-Pillow
Blood-Soaking – My-Sheets

No-Wounds – No-Cuts
What is Happening
God-In-Heaven – Help-Me
I-Fear-The-Devil – Has a Hold of My-Soul

Evil-Thoughts – Saturating-In-My-Mind
So-Many-Evil-People – Will-Die
Death – Will-Have to Speed-Reap
As-The-Dead – Begin to Out-Number – The-Living

God-In-Heaven – Help-Me
I-Fear-The-Devil – Has a Hold of My-Soul
Wait a Moment – Maybe-I'm-Okay
666 is Branded – On-My-Head
Maybe-I'll-Make-It – To-The-End

(Six Earth Months Ago)

(Satan)

Burn-Burn – You-Damned-Souls
Your-Flesh is Fake – All-In-Your-Mind
As it Burns-Away – From-Your-Fake-Bones
While-You-Pray – For-Your-Souls to Die

Hey-Demon – That-Soul-Over-There
Its-Head is Poking – Out of The-Flames
Be a Very-Evil – Demon-For-Me
Stomp-On-It – Until-It-Stays – Submerged

Something is Not so Hellish
In-My-Mind – I-Feel a Little-Bit of Peace
What is This – I-Never-Feel-Peace
Slow-Down-My-Hate – Clear-My-Mind
Now-I-Know – This is The-Spark

(Un-Named Human Male)

Six-Months – **666** On-My-Head
I've-Changed – I'm-Evil
This-World – I-Now-Hate
Wish-I-Didn't – Can't-Help-My-Self
I'm-The-Thing – That-Should-Not-Be

Holy-Places – Burn-My-Soul
Grave-Yards – I-Can-See-The-Dead
That-Are-Stuck – After-Death
On-This-World – That-Is at War

I-Hunt – I-Feed-On – Human-Meat
I-Drink-Blood – As it Squirts
From-Ripped – Open-Wounds
God-Did-Not-Bless-Me – He-Damned-Me
I-Thank-Him – For-My-New-Life

Everyday – Evil-Takes – More of A-Hold
My-Soul-Spits-Venom as My-Heart
Loses-More-Love – With-Every-Beat

58

(SIX EARTH MONTHS AGO)

(God)

My-Angels – Come to Me
I-Feel **666** – Deep-Within-Myself
Surround – Your – God
With-All of Your-Love

My-Angels – Heaven-I-Created
First-For-You – Second-For-Humanity
Now-Heaven is Tainted – For a Second-Time
Satan-Was-The-First – There-Will-Be-No-Third

My-Angels – Cry-For-Humanity
My-Angels – Cry-For-Mother-Earth
My-Angels – Know-What-I-Do
Is-Not-My-Doing – It's-Humanity's

Humanity – I-Gave-Love
Humanity – I-Gave-Hope
Humanity – Always-Kill and War
Humanity – Not-My-Finest-Work

Angel-Daniel – Time to Fly to Hell
Rip a Feather – From-Satan's-Wings
His-Un-Named-Son on Earth
Will-Use-It – As a Beacon
For-Satan to Find – When-He-Crawls – Out of Hell

(Harry – A Pimp In New York City)

Damn-War – Costing-Me-Money
Guess – I'll-Have to Cut-Prices
Ladies-Won't – Be-Happy-About-It
It's-Better – Than-Starving

Look at Mister-Evil – He-Looks-Lonely
I'll-Give-Him – Two-For-One
When-He-Turns – I'll-Stab-Him in His-Back
Damn – My-Life-Sucks – Oh-Well
At-Least – I-Get-Mine – For-Free

Hello – Mr. Lonely – I'm-Harry
These-Are-My-Ladies
Touch-One – Touch-Two
Enjoy as Much as You-Want to Pay
Hurt-Them or Take-More
Than-You-Paid-For
You-Will-Bleed – Like a Stupid-Fool

What-Do-You-Say
Which-One or Two
Do-You-Want to Get to Know

(Un-Named Human Male)

Blood-On-My-Lips
Human-Meat – Stuck-In-My-Teeth
It's-Such a Beautiful – Sunny-Day – In-The-Heart
My-New-Home – New-York-City

Wind-Strikes – My-Face
As a Stranger – A-Pimp
Wants-My-Money – In-Trade for Some-Lust
Perhaps-My-Death – After the Fact

Can't-Kill-Them – In-Day-Light
Have to Intake – Their-Disgust
Wave – Them – Away
Wash-My-Hands – In-Their-Blood
When-The-Moon – Shines-Down-Upon-Me

(Sherman And Beverley)
(Two Junkies Needing A Fresh Fix)

B.) Pain the Pain – I-Need a Hit
I'd-Sell-My-Soul – For-Two
Sherman-You-Bastard – Lover of Mine
I'd-Kill-You – For-Three

S.) You're-In-Pain – Least-You
Don't-Have to Listen to Yourself
Beverley – I'd-Sell-You
For-But a Little-Taste
Now – Get-Off-Your-Ass
We-Need-Money – Right-Away
60

(Sherman And Beverley)

The-World-Hates-Us – We-Are-Addicts
All-We-Need – Is a Fix – If-It-Was-Free
We-Wouldn't – Have to Do – What-We-Have to Do
Every – Single – Day

Here-Comes-One-Now – Damn – He-Looks-Evil
1-2-3 – Let's-Hit-Him – Hard
1-2-3 – Let's-Hit-Him – Fast

(Un-Named Human Male)

Pimps and Hookers – Roam the Side-Walk
Now-Junkies – Are-After-My
Blood and Money – Laughable
I-Should – Rip-Off – Their-Heads

666 – I'm-The-Beast
I'm-Tired of Taking – All-The-World's-Hate
Can't-They-See – I'm-Evil
They-Are-Just – Weak and Sick

(Sherman And Beverley)

Jones-In'-Bad – We-Attack
Victims-Fall – Victims-Bleed
We-Grab – Their-Money
Then-Run to Find a Fix
Simple and Dirty – Everyday
But – Not – Today

We-Are-Addicts – We-Are-Human
What-We-Attacked – Was-Not
The-Eyes of A-Beast – Laid-Upon-Us
As-He-Ripped– Into-Our-Flesh
Throwing-Our – Half-Alive-Bodies
In-The-Middle of The Road

No-Time to Cry as We-Died
Our-Souls – Needing a Final-Fix
As-They – Fall to Hell

61

(One Earth Months Ago)

(Un-Named Human Male)

Hello – Dark of Night – What a Day
The-Bad – The-Evil – The-Hell-Bound
Flock to Me – In-The-Light of Day
Now-That – You-Are-Here
All-That-Goes-Away

The-Bad – The-Evil – The-Hell-Bound
Stay-Clear – From-My-Red – Shining-Eyes
As-I-Hunt – Lurking in The-Shadows
Until-I-Strike – Ready to Feast
On-Prey – That-Kill the Weak

(Lady In Yellow)

Look at Me – I'm-Pretty
I'm-Only-Good – For a Night
Am-I a Fool – Searching for Love
In a World – That-Is at War

What is This – This-Man – This-Beast
Staring at Me – Like-I'm-Eatable
I-Cannot-Look-Away – My-Soul-Fears-Him
My-Heart – I-Do-Not-Know-Why
Wants to Love-Him

(Un-Named Human Male)

Such-Beauty – This-Lady – In a Yellow-Dress
Wipe the Blood – From-My-Lips
I-Have to Know-Her – I-Have to Love-Her
My-Evil-Soul – I-Do-Not – Want to Hurt-Her

I-Touch-Her – Her-Flesh is So-Soft
Her-Lips – Pressed-Against-Mine
I-Love-Her – For-Her – I'll-Find-Peace
No-More-Evil – I'll-Cut-Away
The-*666* – From-My-Head

Thank-The-Heavens – God-Has-Saved-Me
I'm-Blessed – I'm-In-Love – Humanity is Saved
62

(ONE EARTH DAY AGO)

(Lady In Yellow)

His-Touch is So-Cold
He-Grunts and Growls
While-We – Make-Love
Why-Do-I – Love-Him
How-Can-I – Let-Him – Touch-Me

I'm-Weak – My-Soul is Half-Dead
My-Love – Has-Not-Quailed
The-Beast – That-Lies-Within – My-Love
I-Know-Very-Soon – I-Will-Die
My-Love is So-Evil
Our-Love – Cannot-Last-Forever

My-Love is Home – Another-Night's
Hunting is Over-With
He-Stinks – He-Smells of Blood
He-Wants-Me – Underneath-Him
I-Am – Damned

(Un-Named Human Male)

Blood-On-My-Lips
Human-Meat – In-My-Belly
I'm-Still-Evil – Humanity is Damned
What is The-Point – Why-Let-This-Go-On

Come to Me – My-Love – One-Last-Time
We-Will-Make-Love – Then-You-Have to Die

The-Sweet – My-Love is So-Fresh
The-Bitter – Eating-Her-Heart
I-Want to Die – Damn-You-God
I'm-Mister-*666* – I'm-The-End

I-Can-Feel-It – My-Death is Coming-Soon
Satan – The-Fallen-One – Owns-My-Soul
I'm-His-Vessel – While-He's-On-Earth
Damn-The-End – I-Was-So-Young
My-Life – Could-Have-Been so Grand

(PRESENT)

(God)

No-More-Time – Nothing-Left to Say
Death – It is Time to Rest
No-More-Reaping – The-Dead
My-Angels – Fly to Earth
Get-Ready to Bring to Heaven
The-Souls – That-I-Deemed-Worthy
To-Share – Heaven-With-Us

(The People Of Earth)

Fire – In-The-Sky
Oceans – Are-Drying-Up
The-Air is Too-Nasty-Thick
To-Breathe-In

Is-This-The-End
God – Please-Help-Us
Satan-Walks – The-Earth
God – Please-Help-Us – We-Are-Helpless
God – Please-Save – Our-Souls

(God)

My-People of Earth
You-Love-War – You-Love-Death
Evil-Has-Taken-Hold
Of-Your-Precious-Souls

You-Kill – In-My-Name
You-Kill – For-The-Glory of Heaven
Help-You – Save-You
No – I-Give-You – *666*
Satan-Collect – Your-Damned-Souls
Leave-Alone-Those – That-Are-Heaven-Bound

(The People Of Earth)
Please-God – Give-Us – One-More-Chance

(God)
No!
64

(Satan)

Once – I-Was-Beautiful
Once – I-Felt-Heaven's-Bliss
Once – God-Loved-Me
Once – There-Was-No-Hell

Anger-Fuels – My-Rage
I-Hate – Everything
Hell-Is a Stinking-Pit
Full of Pain – Blood and Torment
Humans – Come to Me
My-Number is Now – *666*

War – Humans at War
Look at All – The-Carnage
I-Laugh at Your-Hate
You-Think – You-Can-Bring-Forth
Pain and Death so Mighty
Open-Your-Eyes – Witness-Your-End

(Angel Daniel)

I-Daniel – Just an Angel – Watched as Satan
Ripped-Himself – From-Hell
He-Screamed – He-Roared
He-Smiled – Then-He-Breathed-Fire

Thousands – Burnt-To a Crisp
In a Matter of Moments
Satan – The-Fallen-One – Stomped-His
Might-Hoofs – Down-Upon the Earth

Mighty-Lord – What-Happened-Next
Was-Not-To-Be – Satan-Cracked
Your-Beautiful – Mother-Earth – In-Half
I – We – Could-Do-Nothing
As-Every-Soul – On-Earth – Fell to Hell
Mighty-Lord – We-Could-Not – Even-Save-One

(God)

Angel-Daniel – Dry-Your-Tears – Have-Faith
All-I-Need – Is-Seven-More-Days

65

Discography (Pages 66-70)

Books 1 Through 8 Song Listing
B # = Last Number of a Book
Book One: **Who Am I?** – 1-20
Book Two: **Mind Rockin'** – 21-40
Book Three: **Big Time Love** – 41-60
Book Four: **Love High** – 61-80
Book Five: **Siphon Your Minds** – 81-100
Book Six: **Do You Remember Rock And Roll** – 101-120
Book Seven: **Rock And Roll Bachelor** – 121-140
Book Eight: **The End** – 141-160
(Example) **01.** = Original Numbering – **07.** = Book Numbering

01. I Must Go Away - 07. - Book 1
02. A Race Called Man - 03. - Book 1
03. Across The Sky (Edited Version) - 17. - Book 1
05. Justice (Edited Version) - 34. - Book 2
07. Bleeding My Beast Blood Upon the Floor - **20.** - Book 1
08. I Am Wolf - 18. - Book 1
13. Horny Animal Man **(Bonus S. No Book #)** - Book 7
23. Empty Hands (Edited Version) - 36. - Book 2
26. Me Myself & I - 13. - Book 1
33. Enjoy (The Eye) - 90. - Book 5
38. Darken Our Love (Edited Version) - 27. - Book 2
40. Our Love - 45. - Book 3
41. All I Need - 06. - Book 1
43. Love, Baby Love - 63 - Book 4
45. Cursed Years - 04. - Book 1
47. I'm Dying And It's Raining - 14. - Book 1
49. Rip You Apart While Drinking You Down - 19. - Book 1
54. Speak As One - 16. - Book 1
55. Push Me Away - 44. - Book 3
59. We The People - 15. - Book 1
61. Bam Burn Dead Hell (Edited Version) - 38. - Book 2
64. We Are Here - 31. - Book 2
65. The Church of No God (Edited Version) - 32. - Book 2
66. Sweet Sweet Love - 68. - Book 4
67. Who Am I? - 01. - Book 1
70. Shout (Your Day Will Come) - 02. - Book 1
72. Thickness of Mind - 22. - Book 2
73. Rock And Roll House - 10. - Book 1
74. Hero - 12. - Book 1
75. I'll Be Your Hero - 11. - Book 1
76. Tapped (Edited Version) - 30. - Book 2

77. Why - 05. - Book 1
78. Love Den (Not A Sin) (Single Version) - 08. - Book 1
79. Angel Eyes (Single Version) - 09. - Book 1
80. I Am Dream / Prelude To The Eye - 91. - Book 5
81. Stranger Calling No One - 23. - Book 2
83. Set Loose on Hell (S.L.O.H. #1) - **40.** - Book 2
84. Freaking Zombies Man - 39. - Book 2
86. Through the Flame of a Candle - 29. - Book 2
87. I love You - 26. - Book 2
96. Break Me When You're Done - 28. - Book 2
97. She Let Me Pick Her - 72. - Book 4
98. The Last Rocker - 24. - Book 2

100. Purgatory (20 Steps) (The Single) **(P.F. No Book #)**
105. Dying While Texting - 25. - Book 2
111. 3 Can Corn Man - 35. - Book 2
113. Evil Pill - 37. - Book 2
118. Do You Remember Rock And Roll - 111. - Book 6
122. Mind Rockin' - 21. - Book 2
126. Pets and Monsters - 33. - Book 2
127. You Are My Everything - 46. - Book 3
129. Cave Man - 113. - Book 6
132. She's Got To Be Mine - 62. - Book 4
142. Beautiful - 54. - Book 3
144. Rock Is Good (Take One) **(Bonus S. No Book #)** - Book 6
145. I'm Alive - 142. - Book 8
146. Bounty Hunter - 119. - Book 6
147. 1 G 3 L 6 R 8 X - 154. - Book 8
156. I Can Smell Your Death - 94. - Book 5
157. I Can Sense Your Death - 95. - Book 5
166. Brave Face - 93. - Book 5
168. The Push That Got Away - 131. - Book 7
170. The End - 141. - Book 8
171. It Don't Matter - 103. - Book 6
173. Rock Seem Dead - 102. - Book 6
181. Stain - 104. - Book 6
182. Protector - 86. - Book 5
183. Blind Date #1 - **140.** - Book 7
185. Earth Prisoner (# Way Too Many) - **120.** - Book 6
189. Marked - 158. - Book 8
196. Return To Hell - 114. - Book 6
199. Love - 52. - Book 3
205. Rocking & Rolling - 136. - Book 7
206. Freedom's Mountain - 110. - Book 6

207. Pillow Talk - 69. - Book 4
208. Birth - 96. - Book 5
209. Life - 97. - Book 5
210. Death - 98. - Book 5
211. Misery (Poison Red Potion) - 153. - Book 8
214. Coming Home - 105. - Book 6
216. The Other - 124. - Book 7
217. Catch My Heart - 48. - Book 3
219. The Ghost Of My Long Lost Love - 146. - Book 8
224. I Write The Lyrics (Who Cares) - 117. - Book 6
228. Give Me One Time - 147. - Book 8
229. I Erased My Love (Seven Minutes Ago) - 148. - Book 8
230. My Angel Is Lost - 149. - Book 8
238. Time - 64. - Book 4
239. Stay - 65. - Book 4
240. Dressed Up Like A Diner - 83. - Book 5
243. It's Not Me - 143. - Book 8
249. Long Love Train Ride - 84. - Book 5
250. One Day (The Hard / We Can Do It / Our Time Is Here)
    - 57. - Book 3
252. Roar Out Your Hell - 135. - Book 7
253. The Lovers Of Forever - **60.** - Book 3
257. Love Is Too Slow For Me - 138. - Book 7
260. Peace Freaks (Gift #4 No Book #) - Book 1
261. Ordinary - 50. - Book 3
266. The Big Bang **(Bonus S. No Book #)** - Book 5
287. Power To The Mammals Who Don't Walk On Two Legs
    - 85. - Book 5
294 For My Consumption - 159. - Book 8
298. Too Damn Ugly To Get One **(Bonus S. No Book #)** - Book 7

300. Siphon - 81. - Book 5
313. Coma Made For Me - 82. - Book 5
314. Rock And Roll Bachelor - 121. - Book 7
315. One More Time - 122. - Book 7
319. Let's Be Friends (That Sleep Together) - 76. - Book 4
320. Forget About Our Love - 77. - Book 4
323. Little By Little (Duet) - 43. - Book 3
327. High With Me - 66. - Book 4
328. Two Crazy Lovers - 108. - Book 6
341. Fall In Love With Me - 56. - Book 3
344. Flush It (Stupid Stool Samples) - 118. - Book 6
346. Lady From Space (Love Version) - **80.** - Book 4
350. For I, The Unholy One – **160.** - Book 8

561. Love Comes Back Around - 59. - Book 3
563. If You Need Me - 53. - Book 3
566. So I Broke Your Heart - 130. - Book 7
567. Peace and Death (Gift #2 No Book #) - Book 2
576. I Am The Rock (That Likes To Roll) - 106. - Book 6
578. Smile If You Love Me - 73. - Book 4
579. Rocking The World - 101. - Book 6
580. Rock And Roll House #2 (507 Songs Later) - 116. - Book 6
581. Rock Is Good (Take Two) - 112. - Book 6
583. Crash Landed On Their Planet - 99. - Book 5
584. Humans In Space - **100.** - Book 5
587. Rock Is Good (Take Three) **(Bonus S. No Book #)** - Book 6

666. For I, The Holy One **(Bonus S. No Book #)** - Book 8
666.1 666 (A Hell On Earth Opera)
    (Bonus S. No Book #) - Book 8

777. 777 (Might Not Be In Heaven)
    (Bonus S. No Book #) - Book 8

803. Come On Down To Earth - 151. - Book 8
804. Good Human - 152. - Book 8
816. Late At Night **(Bonus S. No Book #)** - Book 8
818. The Book Of Death And Life - 157. - Book 8
850. Untitled Mind Suite (In Five Parts) - 155. - Book 8
(Blank / Mind Power / Mind Patrol / Mind War / The Gemini One)
856. Failure To Rock **(Bonus S. No Book #)** - Books 6 & 7
(Never Have Sex With A Demon Trilogy: 863-865)
863. Demon Slayer **(Bonus S. No Book #)** - Book 5
864. Demon Lover **(Bonus S. No Book #)** - Book 5
865. Give Me Another Chance God / I'm A Demon Now
    (Bonus S. No Book #) - Book 5
877. Sex Warrior **(Bonus S. No Book #)** - Books 6 & 7
883. What Can I Say - 156. - Book 8
888. I'm Armageddon **(Bonus S. No Book #)** - Book 8
889. Buy Me A Beer (You Bastard)
    (Bonus S. No Book #) - Books 6 & 7

906. I Remember Rock And Roll **(Bonus S. No Book #)** - Book 1
908. Rock My Bone **(Bonus S. No Book #)** - Books 6 & 7
941. It's The Beginning **(Bonus S. No Book #)** - Book 8
942. Who Was I (Jimmy's Song / Shawn's Song) - 145. - Book 8

(Original Version Contents)
Book Eight: The End (Pages 4-82)
(The numbers after the song titles are the original numbering)

(Side One) (Mind Messing With Side)
141. The End (170.)
142. I'm Alive (145.)
143. It's Not Me (243.)
144. I'm The Other You (Mirror – Mirror) (372.)
145. Who I Was (The Second Edition) **I.** Party Time / **II.** Coma #1 &
     Shawn's Song / **III.** Coma #2 & Jimmy's Song (592.) **(New)**

(Side Two) (Ghostly Love & Dark Romance Side)
146. The Ghost Of My Long Lost Love (219.)
(Longing, Loving & Losing 147-149)
147. Give Me One Time (228.)
148. I Killed My Love (Seven Minutes Ago) (229.)
149. My Angel Is Lost (230.)
150. I Really Love You (I Really Hate You) (505.)

(Side Three) (Space & Sci-Fi Side)
151. Come In Earth's Child Number One (201.)
152. Space Ship (Earth's Child Number Two) (246.)
153. Misery (Poison Red Potion) (211.)
154. 1 G 3 L 6 R 8 X (147.)
155. King Monster (190.)

(Side Four) (Gothic & Horror Side)
156. Watching You (188.)
157. The Eyes Of Jade (Tears Of Forever)
     (Watching You Part Two) (591.) **(New)**
158. Marked (189.)
159 For My Consumption (294.)
160. Their Dead Starts To Show (295.)

(Bonus Songs)
Kentucky (In-Breds & Meth-Heads) (609.) **(New)**
The Perfect Pill (610.) **(New)**
Her Batteries Just Ran Out (340.)
For I, The Unholy One (350.)

An Ordinary Day In Hell (Pages 83-99)

Quotes (Original Book Versions)

Book One: Who Am I? & Book Two: Mind Rockin'

Quote #1
Let's Shout It Out and Speak As One.
Mind Rock On, The Gemini One.

Book Three: Big Time Love & Book Four: Love High

Quote #2
Catch my heart and take my Hand
to find yourself some Big Time Love.

Purgatory's Full

Quote #3
Open up your Mind Rockin' Minds to the Cold Hard
Reality that is my Songs & Dreams.

Book Six: Do You Remember Rock And Roll &
Book Seven: Rock And Roll Bachelor

Quote #4
For a Mind Rockin' Good Time, Enjoy Some
Rockin' with the Rock and Roll Bachelor

Book Five: Siphon Your Minds &
The Vegetarian And The Slaughterhouse

Quote #5
Come On In And Let The Gemini One
Siphon Your Mind Rockin' Minds.

Book Eight: The End & An Ordinary Day In Hell

Quote #6

The End Is Here – Sliced Up So Nice
For Your Mind Rockin' Minds.

The Beginning Of The End For Mankind

Along time ago when mankind was free to roam free on this Earth, there were no Gods to warp their minds. Everything was going great, slow, but great, mankind was learning more about themselves and about their Earth and all those that lived on her, every single day. But as rulers are today, they were the same at the beginning of mankind. They smiled and pushed themselves in the front of everybody. When they felt that rush of power they did not want to lose it so they did whatever it took to keep themselves in power, including killing. The poor and the pushed will only take so much for so long, before they rise up and take back their rights and their freedoms.

A very wise and corrupted ruler foresaw that the time for something fantastic had to come to be, No something fantastic had to come to life. This ruler gathered together all his wise men and historians, locked them in a guarded room and told them to invent something fantastic that would make his rule supreme standing beside it, so all the poor would listen to him without question because they were to be made to love and fear this new creation. It took years and years for the first, what was to be called the bible, to be held in this ruler's hands. Many first attempts were met with beatings and executions for the wise men and historians.

With tears in his eyes the wisest of the wise men, brought his ruler this bible for he knew in his mind that this bible would be The End of total free thinking for mankind forever. He was just a few steps away from his ruler, when he screamed, NO! I will not let you do this to our people because this bible will spread like a plague across this planet. He tried to run but he was stopped, the bible was ripped away from his hands and he was killed for his disloyalty. The ruler handed his bible, started to read and with every page turned he smiled more and felt even more powerful, it is now *The Beginning of The End for Mankind.*

2016 – The wise man was correct. Such a long time ago plagues this planet with hate and fear. We cannot change the past however the future has still not come to be. Here's to hoping humanity can live for the day and finally find peace and harmony before The End starts to make a lot of sense.

An Ordinary Day In Hell (Pages 74-90)

This ordinary day starts off with Kayden waking up next to Kelly, the dream he was having fades away and with it the peace he was having while his conscious was dreaming, now that reality sets in, Hell is the only thing on Kayden's mind. Kayden can't complain much, he is the new ruler of Hell after all but the truth is Hell is kinda boring, all there is to do almost all day is torture damned souls with many different kinds of ways to do it. Kayden needs a small respite to help clear his mind, on the heavy task that he has set himself out to do, but that task will be mentioned at another time, for right now Kayden is about to get some information from Mr. Dark, that will allow him to have his small respite on Earth.

"Good morning Kelly, I'm going to the office. I know you had a late night, so why don't you stay in bed for awhile longer? The torturing of souls on Earth and Hell can wait on you for a few hours more," Kayden tells a waking up sexy looking Kelly.

"That sounds great I am so tired," replies a wanting to go back to sleep Kelly.

After morning bathroom time is over Kayden walks out of his home. "Good morning Mr Hart," the gate keepers say in unison to me as I am walking up to them. "Good morning, Larry and Peter, how are the families?"

"Just fine," they say in unison once again with calmness in their voices and fear in their eyes. They both can not wait to open the gates for me so I can go on and away from them, so they can calm down and feel safe once again doing their jobs like they have done every day since I killed the last two gate keepers because they pissed me off. The smell of the outskirts of inner Hell hits my nose like a slap to it, the smell of burning flesh and shit is something that I think I will never get use to, this foul scent is nothing compared to the bowels of Hell where all the damned souls are kept for all eternity, for it is them that provide this damn stink that I hate.

Alice, my sexy secretary is waiting for me with a cup of coffee and my daily newspaper, "Good morning, Mr. Hart," Alice says to me with a great big smile on her face.

"Good morning Alice. My don't you look sexy hot today, definitely going to be enjoying our noon-er," I say to Alice with my smile that just drives her crazy, she is in love with me. And just like if we were on Earth, Alice hates Kelly and of course Kelly hates Alice, even wants me to fire her because Kelly feels like Alice is nothing but a nasty slut, that would do anything to take her place in the bed we share every night. I calm down Kelly with hours of love making every time she gets pissed off about Alice but one day I feel that Kelly will have enough and rip Alice's head clean off her pretty little shoulders.

"Would you like your massage now or do you want to wait 'til after our lunch break? After I please you like that woman of yours never can," Alice asks with such a sweet smile on her face.

"I'm a little tight today so I guess I'll take it now, come on in my office in a few minutes, I want to drink my coffee and read my paper first."

"Anything you want Mr. Hart. I'll just make myself look even better for you so I can get you up while making you feel calm at the same time." Alice turns around and walks away shaking one of the sexiest asses that I have ever seen and bitten. Damn this is some good coffee, don't know how Alice does it, she makes the best tasting coffee in Hell. She must know someone in Heaven that supplies her the water to use, because Hell water smells like piss and makes one nasty tasting cup of coffee.

Fifteen minutes later I'm sitting at my desk with Alice giving my rock hard ruler of Hell body another great rub down, when there is a knock on my office door. Alice says, "Go away," before I can answer the knock. "Mr. Hart it is Mr. Dark. I've got something very important to tell you sir something you have been waiting on for some time now." "Come on in Mr. Dark," I command.

Alice gives her wanting to be alone with me undisturbed look at Mr. Dark, that he laughs off just like every time he walks in on Alice and I, which really pisses her off when we're naked.

"I'll just leave you two alone," Alice says walking away.

"Bring me a coffee and a danish," was her answer from Mr. Dark.

"I'll get those for you right after you lick my boots, ass face," Alice says trying to make Mr. Dark feel small.

"Maybe later, but I'll tell you what, if you bring them to me I'll give you a tip."

"What kinda of tip could you give me, Mr. Dark?"

"Don't be a slut, it makes you look as cheap as the makeup you're wearing," Mr. Dark tells Alice laughing. "I'll be right back with your coffee Mr. Dark!"

"That's more like it." I look at Mr. Dark like what the Hell has gotten into you and I am just about to start laughing about the Earth like moment in Hell that just happened when Alice comes walking back into my office carrying not a cup but the whole pot in her hand. Then with a smile on her face she says loudly, "Here's your coffee ass face," then smashes the coffee pot across Mr. Dark's head, knocking him to the floor.

He grabs his head and says, "You crazy ass bitch I'm going to kick your ass." Then Alice kicks him in his face, after that she grabs my phone off my desk and starts to beat the dead Hell out Mr. Dark.

I say to Alice "Get control of yourself Alice, have you lost your mind? Look at what you did. Mr. Dark is knocked out so now I am going to have to wait 'til he wakes back up to find out what he was going to tell me."

Alice still smiling says to me, "Well then let's just have some fun on top of your desk until ass face wakes back up." Sex break over but it took Alice and I longer than it took Mr. Dark to wake back up. He stepped out without saying a word when Alice said, "Wish all you want ass face, but you will never have it because I am made for the top of the food chain and you're nothing but mid-management. You should feel lucky that you even got to see me like this. Now hurry up and get out of the Big Man's office before you turn us off."

I just laugh enjoying my reign of Hell this day. Dressed and done, Alice leaves, gives me a few minutes then sends in Mr. Dark for his privileged meeting with me, because I am such a busy ruler of Hell. "Mr. Hart, thank you for your time, I have something so great to tell you about."

"Take a seat," I tell him. Mr. Dark looks so out of place compared to how he looked when he came in all fast and got his ass kicked by Alice, for being an asshole to her. Alice is hot, super hot and also just like my sweet Kelly lady, Alice does not take any shit from anybody except from me of course. But I don't really give her any shit because she is so very cool to me and so loving because she loves me. She wishes she was my main lady but being second best, I guess to her is better than not at all. Besides, who in Hell would dare try to get something going on with my piece on the side fine, fine lady, that I almost love? "Well go on and inform me then Mr. Dark my patience is limited."

"Mr. Hart great news! Mr. Wheat has just died and his soul is on ice waiting, per your instructions," says Mr. Dark taking a seat.

"This is great news, I am going to have so much fun messing with this hateful bastard. Sustenance is one thing, humans have to eat and a lot of them like to eat meat. But the unmerciful way he made standard in his slaughterhouse on how the animals were to be slaughtered, well he even pissed me off. I'm going to have fun ripping his soul apart."

"Yes sir Mr. Hart and thank you again for letting me have this chance and allowing me to help you by keeping Mr. Wheat ignorant of the fact that this is the start of his eternity in Hell."

"My pleasure. But remember don't screw up and blow this for me. I want him to think that he is watching, Mr. Floyd, who will actually be me of course, trying his best to live his life with the slaughterhouse on his back and mind. Keep this piece of shit greedy as I have my fun spending a little time on Earth like I am a mortal and checking on my future Hell human soldiers at the same time. I guess I did the right thing answering Mr. Floyd's call out to me, telling me that he would give me his soul if I would help him close down the slaughterhouse. Humans are so stupid. Mr. Floyd gave his soul to me for nothing, for Mr. Wheat's soul was heading here no matter what. All Mr. Floyd accomplished was to bring me Mr. Wheat's soul just a little bit faster. And in doing so, he also gave me a soul that was meant to go to Heaven. Is that all Mr. Dark? Or is there something else you need to inform me of?"

"Well, there are still the constant problems that Rigel Burchill is giving to the daily dealings of Hell," Mr. Dark says to me, still so very concerned that I have not handled him already.

"Don't concern yourself with Rigel Burchill, Mr. Dark. He is doing what I want, even though he does not know it yet. And when he gets stronger, making himself a very strong soldier, I will snatch him up, beat him down, making him become the strongest and most loyal of my generals. I have many, many high level demons as my generals already, Mr. Dark. What I need is a former human that once had a soul that belonged to himself, not another soulless demon that has known nothing but evil since their creation. For without a soul, Mr Dark there is no will to go to that next level or to make you fight harder when the moment everything is on the line. It is that extra, Mr. Dark, that will make Rigel Burchill fight 'til he dies after death unlike the most strongest of demons that when they get in that same spot will tuck tail and take off to save their worthless lives. Anything else, Mr. Dark?"

"There are some small things here and there. Nothing too much of a concern but there is one thing that I think you might want to handle before you go to Earth."

"What is that one thing Mr. Dark?"

"Torture room 383. The head demon torturer, the one you renamed Love. Well sir, Love has taken his namesake to the maximum. Love has ended all torturing. He has stage set in's where all the demons and damned souls of 383 get together and roam around together getting along and having fun. They even have a thing called a love fest where the demons and damned souls get together and (Pause)..."

"They get together and do what Mr Dark?"

"Well sir they all have sex together, acting like they are not in Hell."

"Sounds like fun to me Mr. Dark. What's the problem with them doing these things together?"

"The problem is Heaven sir. More importantly God himself."

"What is he bitching about now Mr. Dark?"

"Mr Hart, sir, God wants this to stop immediately and he wants you to be the one to take care of this problem yourself. A.S.A.P."

"Oh does he now?" "Yes sir. The order came down from Heaven this very morning."

"Well you send God a message from me Mr. Dark. Tell God that he can kiss my ass." "Sir?"

"You heard me Mr. Dark. Tell him to kiss my ass."

"Sir please don't make me do that. The last person that sent a message like that to God, well God came down to Hell with that message in hand and shoved it up that person's ass then he pulled it out and then he stuck it down his throat."

"Yeah that was funny as Hell. God was so pissed off at me he didn't talk to me for almost a year. I loved the silence and the non-interference and I wouldn't mind another year of the same thing. So I guess, your ass is toast, huh, Mr. Dark? Don't shit yourself Mr. Dark, I'm just messing with you, you should look at the expression on your face, it's priceless. Okay send God this message, that I will take care of 383 before I go to Earth. Oh yeah, add Hugs & Kisses at the end to freak him out a little bit. I'll get another one of his, I want you one on one, Ready? Type of meetings where I just show up where he wants no matter what I'm doing. I've had my ass bare many times, God just laughing telling me to suffer as he pulls me away from a special moment that I was enjoying, with one of my many, many fine evil ladies or lady demons, those that shine in Hell shines so sexy bright that they illuminate where you're standing next to them. It feels like a warm sexy light from Heaven. I bask in it Mr. Dark. As I look into your eyes and into the soul that I allow you to keep, I ask myself, do you enjoy having it or is it more of a curse?"

"Working for me with a soul, doing the things that you do for me, you're very good Mr. Dark just like I wanted you to be. I wanted someone from Earth that could be soulless with a soul all snuggled up all safe inside them. You're my number one, it's time to step things up. When we're doing our Hell on Earth things you got to take it easy, feel that soul you have inside you, let it guide you. I need a friend on Earth, someone that can bring it to me, make me believe the things you say to me, as I and we mess with many more damned souls that just entered Hell. Like this next one, this Mr. Wheat. I want you to make him feel like he is the most important soul that has entered Hell. When he feels himself rising, his soul heading back to Earth, he will be so happy, then

I will reach out, grab his soul, slap it around a little, then I'm going to take this crap of a soul, head first I tell you, and dip it in the big pit of burning shit. I will watch as his soul tries to escape, then I'll pick up a stone, throw it on top of him, weighing him down, with a snap of my fingers that stone will digs itself inside this worthless soul, making it sink to the bottom of the burning shit pit. So in the long about route that I just took you, Mr. Dark, you need to be a Big A not a Big D if you know what I mean. You do know the difference, Mr. Dark?"

"I think so?"

"What do you mean I think so? I read your file, you got a lot of ass on Earth, no where as much as I did of course, you're like junior league compared to me, but that is neither here nor there. You were after one thing, you got it then got going, not sticking around to break their hearts. I like that, Mr. Dark, so let yourself go and go get laid. Tell you what, you go to Earth, have a good time I'll be there as soon as I finish with 383."

"Mr. Hart, thank you sir."

"Well don't just sit there thinking about it Mr. Dark go get to doing it and on the way out send Alice back in here, I got a few more minutes to spare. Think I'll let 383 have their last whatever before I come in and smash and thrash, destroying everyone there, chop them all into very small pieces of final death, then watch as my sweeping and scooping demon minions take their remains to the center of Hell. Laughing as they dump those remains into the living, feeding, flames of Hell, rejoicing as the flames grow brighter, higher and hotter. It's good to be the ruler of Hell, Mr. Dark. This Hell, my Hell! feeds me power, now that I rule, I fear no one or nothing in my Hell. Pawns all of you, nothing more, to do with as I please. I'm a big A, using my Hell power where I may. Not like I'm told, how Satan was, it appears Satan was one great big D to the beings that lived in his Hell."

"So be very damn happy that I now rule, for I know Satan would have enjoyed ripping you apart, while dangling your soul above you, just out of hands reach forever."

"Mr. Hart you're the best. Beep Satan, Satan who? You're the man Kayden Hart. Sir, I feel blessed that you gave me this chance, I owe you everything, my soul, the one that you allow me to have, it feels so

80

good inside me, makes Hell a whole lot more bearable. Even though I have to do some very Hellish things, my soul keeps me strong in letting me remember that I am not them, being Helled on forever and Mr Hart, sir that makes me so very happy."

"Good, that's very good Mr. Dark. Now stop trying to kiss my ass, your nose is getting brown. Ha ha. Leave now, send in my little cute witch hottie."

Alice walks in with a smile on her face, "That dried blood looks so good on ass face's head, I almost made him bleed again," Alice says taking off her clothes after closing the door.

"You know Alice, I like that I found you in Hell, your torture was very much for failing Satan when you failed to seduce me in Purgatory."

Alice pauses walking and taking off her clothes, "Kayden you know I hate when you bring that up. I was so hot looking and you tied me up and was getting ready to kill me when I screamed for Satan and that bastard sent me here to Hell where I was stuck in a pit filled with snakes, spiders, all kinds of bugs and so many ugly, ugly men with boils on their faces, that constantly oozed out puss. They would hold me down and kiss me all over my body, then they would eat me alive then I would reappear only to try to run away from them and all the other nasty things in my own private Hell that was made for me all because of you. Kayden you bastard, I hate you for making me live through my Hell, but I love you even more for pulling me out of it. Kayden may I show you how much I love you?"

"Come and get your taste sweet Alice."

(One hour later) "Kayden, may I ask you something?" "Ask away Alice."

"When I came up to you in Purgatory with that bone in my mouth trying to freak you out and seduce you at the same time," "Yeah?" "Why did you save me by pulling that bone out of my throat? Why didn't you just let me choke to death and walk away?"

"Like you know Alice, I was weak and on guard, I saved you and tied you up so I could know what you wanted and see if there was anyone else with you."

"Kayden there's one more thing I have to know." "And what is that Alice?"

"Kayden, my sweet Kayden, if you were not in such a hurry to make yourself stronger by absorbing that witch's lost power up, if you had the time, would you have made love to me?" Kayden smiles loving his power over Alice, "Alice I would have made love to you for the rest of the day."

"Thank you Kayden, that means the world to me, I just couldn't live with myself if I thought that I turned you off. Kayden?"

"What now Alice?" "Can we make love one more time before you get demon's blood all over your hands and then go back to that slut of yours Kelly to make love to her before you go to Earth for your vacation?"

"Can't get enough of me Alice?" "Never," Alice replies retaking off her clothes.

Another hour later, Kayden is sitting at his desk naked, and coming up with an idea for some lyrics he is going to use when he sings them out loud to Mr. Wheat. Kayden finishes then asks Alice to listen to his new lyrics as he sings them out to her. After Kayden is finished singing he is all fired up from the power he got from singing them out loud. Alice smiled and cheered telling Kayden that he is the best, that no one, but no one could come up with lyrics and sing them like that, so intensely as to make the person that their meant for feel them and feel them deeply.

I Slaughter – The Slaughterhouse
The Old Damn Bastard – Is Dead
He Died While Killing Animals
One Moment With Blood On His Hands
He Grabbed His Chest – Then He Died – Then I Won The War
No More Blood! – No More Blood!
The Slaughterhouse Is Closed Forever

If The Old Damn Bastard Wants Forgiveness
He Can Kiss My Alive Ass – To Death
I Hate Him & I'm Glad – That He Is Dead
I Hope He Is Burning In Hell
I Hope He Feels Like One Of The Animals He Killed
I Slaughter – The Slaughterhouse **(13)**

Kayden is about to get dressed, when a thought for some more lyrics comes to him, this time these lyrics will be given to Mr. Dark to give them to Mr. Wheat, so Mr. Wheat will feel even more confident and secure when he sings them out to Kayden as he is playing the role of Stan Floyd. Once again Kayden asks Alice what she thinks of them, this time Alice has no smile on her face instead Alice has a look of pure fearful terror on it. Kayden smiles and says, "Beep yeah."

I Come To Eat Your Soul To Death
You Vegetarian Bastard
Then – Ha Ha
I'm Going To Make You
Eat Bloody Raw Meat
Right Off The Living Never Dying Animals
That You Will Eat Forever

While Rotting & Screaming &
Bleeding & Burning In Hell
I Am Your Hell Tormentor
Your Forever Bringer Of Pain
Get Ready To Die Bad & Burn In Hell
You Horrible Vegetarian Bastard (13)

Kayden is getting dressed watching Alice leave his office, with a mix of love and fear in her eyes. After she closes the door Kayden huffs out, "I rule Hell. Satan was weak. Satan has no Meat or balls. I'm all man. I'm all devil. God you better fear me. One day God. One day, the end."

Kayden is now walking the halls of Hell, walking by demons that greet him with fear and respect. Kayden is talking to himself, "Well it looks like Love the demon shall be no more. I had a great time molding him into the peaceful, love filled demon that he is today. He was lost, questioning himself. After the fall of Satan, he looked to me for guidance and I gave him something that did not fit in Hell making him feel like he was so very special. Yeah, I did this as a slap to the face of God, showing him that even in Hell, there can be things like love and peace. And wouldn't you just know it, God hates this idea, makes his Heaven look a little bit less grand and less one of a kind for its glorious goodness and heartfelt feelings. Here it is torture room 383, so different sounding from the outside compared to the rest of the torture rooms. No screams, no pleas, no chopping sounds. No what I hear is singing in the air, everyone sounds so very happy, too bad for them. What can I do? I have to re-welcome them back to Hell then kill them all."

I turn the knob of door 383 just enough to open it up, I take a breath then I kick the door all the way open slamming it against the inside wall. Screams fill the air as I roar out Hell from my being. I do not want to do this, I like Love, he's a great and gentle demon, that likes to spread out the word of my name. For to him my name means goodness, Love loves me for setting him free. Now Love stares at me with pleading eyes of no please don't. Then when he sees no mercy in me, Love tries his best to bring out the demon that he was, but to no avail. Love does not have hard evil inside himself anymore. He cries in anger of his weakness unable to save all the good people of love room 383. I roar out again for Love to come to me, to accept his fate, to kneel down in front of me so I can rip off his head with my bare hands. This is not my fault I am not the trigger I am just the bullet this time, I strike whomever I am pointed at. Sometimes Hell does suck, even for the ruler of it.

Love does not come to me instead he takes the claws on his right hand and scratches at his face making it bleed. Love then licks the blood off his claws in an attempt to rage up. So damn laughable, bring it on Love. Love runs at me like he is the most ferocious demon that lives in Hell. Love is so wild, so intense looking running towards me, I see the look of victory in his eyes. Good for you Love, go out of existence with love in your heart and the fury inside you to defend the rights of all your good people of love room 383.

Love hits me hard, full of rage just enough to back me up a few inches, his killing fist shots make me bleed, but I am so powerful I heal just as fast. Love does not stand a chance, I grab Love by the throat. The noise of damned souls and demons trying to escape turns to silence as they all stop in union watching me with my hand around their spiritual leader. I look at them with nothing but an empty void in my eyes. They start to cry and beg me not to kill Love. Then out of nowhere a damned soul with a wonderful voice starts to sing this happy song. Then like magic, love room 383 is filled up full with hundreds of voices singing together this happy song. I stop, letting go of Love. Cheers fill the air then I put my fist straight through Love's face, all the way through to the back of his head. The cheers turn to crying again as they watch me pull my fist back out of Love's head, then with horror they watch as I take hold of the hole I made and pull at it until Love is torn completely in half by my cold and steady evil hands.

"Curse you! Curse you! You killed Love! – Off with his head! – Death to Kayden Hart! – You're just as bad as Satan! – Long live Love!"

The mob turns very angry, the sobs that lasted only moments after I killed Love, turn to rage very quickly. I stand still with all the power of Hell inside me, ready to destroy everything inside this room. Helpless fools, all of them. I don't hate them, I almost love them. Why is this happening? Because their time is up, they are a success in Hell but a failure to Heaven. There is no such thing as fun in Hell, that is the saying and that is my command, that I wipe my ass to everyday. I may be God's hand picked Devil, for whatever his reason and I'll do his bidding. I'll get the job done un-sloppily, but after I am done, after I wipe the blood away from my being, I will party, I will have a great time and yes I will get laid. If God does not like this, he can kiss my ass and give this Hellish evil gig to someone else. My comply only goes so far no matter who I'm giving my comply to, I gotta be me.

The mob of hundreds of damned souls and demons run screaming at me, wanting my blood, wanting my death. The first to strike, strike at nothing, as I move myself out of harm's way, with but a blinking of my eyes. I am the last being in line of this angry mob, I reach out to bring pain and death, so very easy to these damned souls that squish between my fingers, the demons take a little longer, but not much more. Getting caught up in the moment, I roar out, "Fools, fools, what can you do? Nothing, for I am Kayden Hart, the new Devil of Hell. I rule, I feel pain and it makes no difference. I heal from wounds of death. All your might together is for naught, you all will die. Fight harder, strike deadlier, make me feel your pain and loss. I love it, it feeds me, makes me want to keep on fighting the good fight. 'Til the day I receive my damn wings, I fight for my right to be in Heaven, all you fight for is your worthless lives that mean nothing compared to my blessed and un-blessed soul."

I spit at the no wind, raging up to end this even faster, the blood that is spilled splashes all the way to the ceiling. I look up watching the blood flow come back down on me like bleeding rain. I keep on ripping and tearing away at my prey, wondering if God is watching me. I stop, half of love room 383 is now empty. I shake my head, damn this sucks. I don't feel like killing anymore and I watch as confused walking away occupants of love room 383 pray that the blood slaughter is over with. I try to rage them up and make them attack me again but the fight is out of them. So I wipe away the tears from my eyes and start humming a tune that will take my mind off what I am doing 'til I finish.

I smile that it is over with, the last one to die lays at my feet dead. I roar out my command and twenty or more of my sweeping and scooping demon minions enter torture room 383 to clean it up and dispose of the waste, so once again it can be filled full of demons that torture the damned souls that are assigned to it, just like all the other 665 torturing rooms. I have to take a shower but first I want to drink down some beer and smoke some weed. I walk down the halls of Hell once again on my way to Styx Bar & Grill. I walk in, blood soaked, feeling like Hell, glasses clink together as I am welcomed by the drinkers and smokers that like to have a good time. One of my usuals, Becky comes up to me smiling, having a good buzz going. Becky's smile fades fast as she looks me in my eyes, "Kayden are you alright?" a concerned Becky asks me. I don't answer her, I just keep walking up to the bar, turned around buzzing, demons look at me, then scatter away like scared children trying to get away from the boogie man.

"I want a bucket of beer and some of Hell's finest green funk," I command to the bartender. "Right away Mr. Hart, sir, right away." I'm handed a pitcher of beer and a glass, I grab the pitcher up then smash the glass on the floor. I down the whole pitcher of beer like it was but one glass. I demand, "Another and no glass. You hand me another glass and I will smash it across your head this time. Now hand me my weed, it better be the best." I'm smoking away, when my new pitcher of beer arrives, the very nervous bartender spills some of it on the counter. I look at him watching him squirm, praying to himself that I don't kill him over spilled beer. I look him in the eyes and blow smoke in his face, grab my beer and walk away. I hear his relief from behind me and without spilling a drop of my beer, I turn back around and rip him apart just for the Hell of it.

Becky comes back up to me after I finish my second pitcher of beer and my giant bowl of weed. I'm feeling a whole hell of a lot better. Becky's smile returns seeing this in my eyes. "Kayden?" I just look at her. "Kayden, are you alright now?"

"No but I feel better. What do you want Becky?"

"I want to make you smile Kayden. You look like you could use my company for awhile." I nod my head yes and Becky starts to take off my blood soaked clothes. Everyone at Styx Bar and Grill watches as the beautiful Becky wipes the blood off my face, hands and body. I try to get turned on but hate is still full in my mind, so I click it away the best I can and enjoy myself for awhile.

86

When we're done, Becky is begging for more as I walk away done with her and don't want any more. Becky's cries fill my ears as I walk back up to the counter to order another pitcher of beer. I finish it, then walk out the door naked heading to my home in Hell, to a maybe still sleeping Kelly.

I walk inside my home, look in on Kelly who is still sleeping, I look at her for a few minutes then I walk away to take a shower. I wash and I wash, taking my time letting the water cleanse my body as my soul and mind remain scarred and dirty, like they will always be forever. I'm very hungry all of a sudden, so I walk back to Kelly and I wake her up by laying beside her and pulling her closer to me, feeling her warm body, Kelly feels like Heaven in my arms. Kelly smiles at me then gives me a kiss. "What's going on Kayden?"

" I'm a little hungry and I thought I'd ask you if you are as well?"

"Yes I'm a little hungry, I could eat something small." Kelly looks at me closer, "Kayden, are you alright?"

I just laugh out loud getting up at the same time, "Yeah I'm fine Kelly, just having one of those days."

"What do you want to eat, I feel like having some scrabbled eggs, toast and coffee," Kelly tells me still concerned. "How about you Kayden, what are you going to have?"

"I feel like having a salad with some fruit on the side and a bottle of wine." Kelly just smiles at me and says, "Make that two Kayden."

We finish our meals and wine, Kelly takes a shower, comes up to me with a towel wrapped around her head and body when she is done. I unwrap her, loving how her naked body looks. Kelly smiles at me, wanting to make love to me as much as I want to make love to her. When we are finished, we walk together hand in hand to take a shower together. Kelly washes my body as I cry and roar out my pain of the day. I tell Kelly how I had to kill Love the Demon, with tears in her brown eyes, she forgives me for killing one of her best friends, then asks me if I had to kill Peace the Demon his twin brother as well. Not yet but his time will come one day very soon, God will see to that for sure. We get dressed slowly talking about what Kelly is going to be doing when I am away on Earth.

Giving Kelly a goodbye kiss, I tell her to be ready when I need her to play her part on Earth. I also tell her to make sure one more time that everybody I am using for this little bit of fun for me and a very big kick in the mind for this monster of a soul, Mr Wheat, will be ready when their part comes up and not to screw it up. I tell her to especially make sure that Samantha, Lara and Tracie are more than ready, I want them to bring it out real, like they are the part they are playing, for a watching Mr. Wheat.

Kelly tells me that Samantha is not happy that she is being pulled out of her torture room and away from her favorite thing, torturing the souls of bad men, to play the role of his dream lady. I tell Kelly to remind Samantha that she owes me for all the shit I had to take from her while we were together in Purgatory. I also tell her to remind Samantha that I know just how much she likes to play the part of a sexy lady Librarian that only wants to make the man that wants her pay for his lust of her with lots of pain, so she is perfect for this role as my dream lady. Thinking to myself, I remind myself to tell Kelly to tell Lara to put on extra makeup because she has to look as much alive and non-evil as she can.

I am about to tell her good bye when Kelly asks me if I could sing her a sad song before I leave. I smile at her and walk away to grab my guitar, I pick it up and walk back over to Kelly. I sit on the bed with my guitar in my hands, I pause to think up something new. A smile comes to my lips and I start singing and playing my guitar to a new song that I come up with for my sexy Ex-Hell Witch, now my present number one lover in Hell.

The End Of Love

Wondering to Myself
If-I'm – Making a Mistake
My-Heart-Tells-Me – That-I'm-Not

My-Love – That is Inside-Me
Feels so Cold and Alone
I-Know – What-I-Must-Do
Hoping – Deep – Down
That-I-Will – Find-Love – Once-Again

(Chorus)
When There's Nothing Left To say
When The Breaking Of Two Hearts
Brings The End Of Love
The Pain Of Loss Sinks In
Scarring Two Souls at Once

I-Loved-You so Much – My-Love
But-Now – That-Love-Lies
Dead – Inside – Me
I-Know – Wishing-Will-Not
Bring-It-Back to Life

So-I-Open-Up – My-Eyes
Letting-You – Fly-Away
Free and Alone – Just-Like-I-Am

(Chorus)
When There's Nothing Left To say
When The Breaking Of Two Hearts
Brings The End Of Love
The Pain Of Loss Sinks In
Scarring Two Souls at Once

I look up at Kelly, she is so beautiful, with tears falling from her brown eyes, from my sad song "The End Of Love". I feel sad as well and I don't want to go to Earth with this song playing in my mind so I tell Kelly to hold on for a moment while I play another new song as soon as I think it up first and for her to get ready to dance around like she is still alive.

89

Dance

Come-On-Kelly – My-Fine-Lady
It's-Time to Wipe – Away-Your-Tears
Hell – Sucks so Bad

Let's-Stop-Letting it Bring-Us-Down
Like-We-Have – No-Souls-Inside-Us
Instead-I-Say to You – My-Fine-Lady

(Chorus)
Let's Dance & Dance
& Dance Some More
I Want To Feel Alive
Holding You In My Arms
Swinging You Around
So Let's – Dance & Dance
& Dance Some More

Come-On-Kelly – My-Fine-Lady
It's-Time to Wipe – Away-Your-Tears
Hell – Sucks so Bad

Let's-Stop-Letting it Bring-Us-Down
Like-We-Have – No-Souls-Inside-Us
Instead-I-Say to You – My-Fine-Lady

(Chorus)
Let's Dance & Dance
& Dance Some More
I Want To Feel Alive
Holding You In My Arms
Swinging You Around
So Let's – Dance & Dance
& Dance Some More

"Hey Donna, come on over baby so we can ****. Don't forget to bring the 'Book Of Hell' with you when you come to enjoy me."

"Kayden, I don't know about this? I'm scared."

"Scared of ****ing me? Or about our adventure dabbling with Hell?"

"What do you think Kayden?"

"Hard choice Donna. You've cursed my **** for being so all that. Hell might seem like calm waters to you?"

"Very funny Kayden, I don't want to drive over there, come pick me up."

"I can do that Donna but I was planning on getting ****ed up then **** you. Then play with some Hell, then maybe **** you again, then crash out 'til morning, so you will have to stay the night and sleep in the love spot."

"You bastard Kayden!" "Why does every woman I ****, eventually call me a Bastard?"

"Because you are one Kayden, I don't even know your last name. You just showed up out of nowhere wanting my 'Book Of Hell'. I said no. You seduced me. I let you because you are so damn good looking. Even now Kayden, I want to tell you no, you cannot have my 'Book Of Hell'. I can not resist you, even though you will break my heart by taking yourself away from me. Kayden, I will still bring you my 'Book Of Hell' to own."

"That's my Donna. And you are completely right, but what a night you will have Donna. I promise to make our last night together one you will never forget. Now drive over here and bring me my book and your body Donna or I'll start without you."

"Don't you dare Kayden, I'll be over there as soon as I can, I love you Kayden."

"I know you do Donna, and I love your body. And one more thing Donna, bring some tacos or a pizza."

"Anything else I can bring you Kayden?!"

"Yeah Donna a bottle of great Scotch and a sack of weed."

"What Kayden?" "Kidding about the weed just bring the Scotch." "I was going to say Kayden."

"Don't tell me Donna that your hung up on weed. There are people that are starving, there are people getting killed, what is smoking some weed compared to that?"

"Nothing, I guess Kayden. I'm sorry, I wasn't thinking."

"Donna I'm just messing with you, now bring your fine ass over here so I can give you something that you will never have again your whole life."

"I love you Kayden." "Don't go breaking your own heart Donna." Click.

(In Hell) "Kelly I'm going to Earth for a few hours."

"Why Is it that Kayden? To see that Earth bitch Donna again?"

"No Kelly, I'm not going to see her, I'm going to **** her and finally get my hands on the 'Book Of Hell'."

"Kayden you're a Bastard."

"Yeah, yeah, Kelly I know, now tell me you love me, so very, very much."

"Kayden come here you lovable bastard and **** me before you go." "Just take off your clothes Kelly."

92

(On Earth) Kayden Hart's apartment, one of many, throughout time, thanks to the 'Blood Stone'. Donna, to herself, "Come on Donna, you got to step up your game girl if you want to keep a man like Kayden or better yet be allowed to share his bed. It's time to fold in your wings and get ready to do a lot of sinning." Donna entered Kayden's apartment, nervous, excited, and ashamed. Kayden with his large sexuality had Donna in his bed within fifteen minutes. Donna purred. Donna cried. Kayden enjoyed giving her all the emotions that she has not felt since? All because of her situation.

"Kayden, do you really want and enjoy me? Or was all this because of a book?"

"Both Donna. I would have done anything to get my hands on this book that you gave me. And thank you again, Donna. I saw and felt that you wanted me and needed to have a love explosion enter your life. You are a beautiful woman Donna, it was my pleasure to give you what you always wanted but has been denied to you for too long. The answer is yes, Donna, if you did not have this book and wanted me for some great loving. I would have said yes, wanting to enjoy you very much. For like I said you are a beautiful, sexy, woman, with a body that feels untouched."

"Kayden stop it, your embarrassing me."

"I know, I love my power over you. Can you handle more of my loving, Donna? Or do you want me to get to making something happen with my new 'Book Of Hell' that I now own? Donna?"

Donna is shaking with the fear of betrayal going through her mind, while holding something hidden behind her back. "You don't have to if you don't want to Donna."

"Yes I do Kayden!"

"No you don't. Fully give yourself to me Donna and you can stay with me as one of my many lovers and mistresses."

"Part of me would love to Kayden, but you are evil, the new ruler of Hell, I have come to kill you."

"Kill me Donna? Don't over step your reach, beautiful, golden Angel."

"You knew, Kayden? How could you know? I played my part perfectly?"

"Perfectly, Donna? Come on, the touch of you is so pure. I know that kind of touch very well Donna, for I have felt it once before, so many long years ago. You have the feel of Heaven inside you. That Donna, you can never hide."

"You bastard Kayden!" Donna in a rage brings forth a knife from behind her back and thrusts it toward Kayden, with a killing strike to his heart. Kayden waits 'til the last second and stops Donna's killing attempt, then takes the knife out of her hands and places it on the bed. With Donna weak and scared, Kayden grabs a hold of her, pulls her close to him, kisses her deeply, then makes love to her with a knife that can perhaps kill him in reach of Donna's hands at all times, which she never grabs and uses, for greed has entered her being and she wants Kayden to darken her soul so that Heaven will be denied to her, so God will send her to Hell with Kayden to feel like this forever.

"Do you trust me Donna?"

"Yes Kayden, yes."

"Then let me tie you up and release you of all that Heaven's light you have inside that fine angel body of yours."

"Yes Kayden, please, I love you, I want to be with you forever." Kayden ties up Donna the Angel, then laughs out loud, a laugh that can only come from Hell itself.

"Kayden what are you doing? Untie me right now! Kayden Please don't do this to me!"

"Stupid, horny Angel of lust, look at what you got yourself into!"

"I'll rip out your heart, Kayden Hart, you bastard."

"With what hands Donna, the ones that are confined by chains from Hell? Let me show you how much control I have, over you Donna." With a snap of his fingers the chains that bind Donna's body start to burn her with the flames of Hell. Donna screams, crying from the pain of her confinement.

"Please Kayden no more!"

"Okay Donna, I'm not that evil, yet! What to do with you now? I know my 'Book Of Hell' I'll use it to send you to Hell, very, very painfully. How does that sound to you Donna?"

"I am an Angel, I am too pure for Hell."

"Not anymore Donna, all that lust you crave and still crave makes you a perfect candidate for my Hell."

"I don't lust you Kayden, I hate you! Untie me and I will show you just how much I hate you right now, you bastard."

"Liar, liar, Donna. I'm the all that, you cannot get in Heaven and you know it. Nothing to say Donna? That's probably for the best, you better save as much strength as you can for your painful trip to Hell. Now hold still Donna, while I read this enchantment. I like to say to you Donna, that I am sorry for the pain that you will feel. But that would be a lie, I'm going to enjoy having my own fallen angel to own in my Hell, to use as my plaything. Don't shake your head no, Donna. This is exactly what you want!"

"Like Hell it is, you piece of Hellish monster from Hell."

"Sticks and stones Donna. When you get to Hell Donna, I want you to clean up and be ready for me upon my return."

"No! Kayden, No!" "Yes! Donna, Yes!"

With victory in his voice, Kayden speaks out the enchantment, and nothing happens. Now it is Donna's time to laugh.

"Kayden, you dumb, evil bastard! Your world is just about to come apart all around you," says Donna with lots of satisfaction in her voice. Kayden looks at Donna with confusion as the door to his apartment comes crashing open, surprising Kayden, making him look over and see the Voice of God standing there with a big smile on his lips.

Voice: "Kayden, Kayden how have you been, you piece of human ass trash?"

Kayden: "Hung like the ruler of Hell. How have you been, no balls?"

Voice: "Always full of humor. Well this time the joke is on you, Kayden! It might not be "April's Fools Day", but still you are the fool anyway Kayden. For that book you hold in your hand is nothing but a lie that I spread so you would search and search for it, wanting the power it holds for yourself. How does it feel to be a fool Kayden?"

Kayden: "Bravo, bravo, Voice, you sack of crap. No shit it's a book of lies. Just look at you Voice, standing there like a jackass, not knowing what's going on. This look is perfect for you, no balls."

Voice: "What are you talking about, Human scum?!"

Kayden: "I'll tell you Voice but before I do take this." Kayden with quickness, runs towards the Voice of God, and clothes-lines him down on his ass. "That's for my door, no balls. Stay down or I will knock you back down, better yet kneel to me Voice."

Voice: "Never, human scum, I'd rather die first!"

Kayden: "That can be arranged Voice, very easily. Nothing? That's what I thought, you no ball, limp Angel of nothing's happening."

Voice: "This time you have gone too far Kayden. This was my ass to your face, for all the shit I have taken from you. It has taken me some years of contemplation to finally realize that you Kayden Hart are nothing but a pretty faced monster. A bully to me and I am not going to take any more from you, human scum." The Voice of God, stands on his feet in defiance to Kayden.

Kayden: "Voice, Voice, what have you made yourself believe that you can do to me? You are the fool Voice, I will be the one that always wipes my ass on your face, you're a pathetic, waste of a pair of wings. Which makes me think I still want my wings, and who says my wings can't have been owned already, once. Voice, your wings look pretty good to me, just a little jagged from the time I tried to pull them off you in Purgatory. Since you're being so stupid Voice, I say no time like the present to rip them all the way off you, since big brother is not here to save your soon to be wingless carcass from another beat down."

Voice: "Bring it on."

Kayden: "Bring it on, is that all I get? I've been talking for five minutes here and you give me, Bring it on? I'll bring it on no balls, damn what a fool you are!"

Voice: "Wait a minute, Kayden, think about what you are doing. "

Kayden: "Hesitation, first sign of weakness, you've already lost." Kayden, with no intent to carry out his said plan, gets ready to smack the Voice of God around, then kick his ass back to Heaven. When lightning in a bottle strikes inside Kayden's apartment, blinding everyone with the Light of God. Kayden smiles, The Voice still prays, Donna the Angel, is still tied up.

(God's words spoken out) "Kayden, every time I feel there is hope for you, you do something like this. My Voice should feel like a brother to you, and you My Voice, you should be thankful of Kayden. For if it were not him as the new Ruler of Hell, then someone else would have taken his place, perhaps you. How would you like to live in Hell, My Voice? I want no more of this between you two."

Kayden: "How about it Voice do you want a hug?"

Voice: "Kiss my ass, you."

(God) "Voice!"

Voice: "I am sorry, my Lord, please forgive me."

Kayden: "Sickening, why don't you just have your lips permanently placed on God's Ass, Voice."

(God) "Kayden! I said Enough! Don't make me punish you by coming to Hell and killing all your women, and I mean all of them, Kayden!"

Kayden: "Alright, alright, God, don't give yourself gas."

(God) "What!? Why you little Devil you, take this and take that." God reaches down from Heaven, grabs hold of Kayden, picks him up, then slams him through his apartment floor. Then God grabs a hold of Kayden and does it all over again. "You done with your attitude now Kayden?" Kayden is bleeding lots of blood, with many of his bones protruding from his body.

Kayden: "In the end God not even close, but for right now yeah. Enjoy your victory."

(God) "Victory? There was not even a challenge to obtain victory. This you better keep in mind Kayden for I am the Almighty and you are simply just one of my many servants."

Kayden: "I'm under your skin"

(God) "What was that Kayden?"

Kayden: "Nothing, God."

(God) "That's better, now untie my Angel, she needs to come home to Heaven to have the taint of Hell cleansed from her."

Kayden: "You sure you want her back God? She is more than just tainted. I don't want to push things, God, but I know women. If you take her away from me, she will mope around Heaven longing to be with me." (Silence) "God?"

(God) "You sicken me Kayden. Have her then, I guess Voice you are going to have to find a new girlfriend".

Kayden: "She's your girlfriend, Voice? Ha, ha, ha, ha, you are so pathetic, Voice. You sent your woman to seduce me, you with nothing that can satisfy her."

Voice: "Shut your damn mouth! I hate you!"

Kayden: "Right back at you, Voice. God, you have to give me this one, this is too great to pass up."

(God) "What do you want, Kayden?"

Kayden: "Just to sing out, one song to the Voice."

(God) "Alright, but it better be a good one."

Get It Up (Page 95 of Purgatory's Full)

Don't – Forget to Look – When-You
Do-Your-Flushing in Heaven
Because in Your-Bowl – Might-Be
The-Voice of God
Eating-Up – All the Crap
That-You – Just-Crapped-Out

Go-Voice – You're the One
The-More-Crap – You-Dish-Out
The-More – I-Will-Make-You – Eat-Up
You're-Nobody's-Friend and a Liar
Such a Damn – No-Ball-Bastard
Because – You-Can't-Ever – Get-It-Up

Voice: "I'll kill you Kayden you! (Lots and lost of four letter words.)"

Kayden: "Shut up, Mr. Limpy, before your words get you sent to Hell. A Hell that I rule, where I will make you lick the bowels of it."

Voice: "Not if I kill you first!"

(God) "Hold steady my Voice. Kayden?" (Silence)

Kayden: "God?" (Silence)

(God) Ha, ha, ha, ha, ha, ha, ha, ha, ha, ha. "Damn! Kayden you are a real bastard, a real Devil, now go back to Hell." Ha, ha, ha, ha, ha. "You know my Voice, that song does resemble you. You have a habit of giving out a lot of crap and a lot of Heaven's Angles give you a lot of crap back in return. Maybe you should change your ways."

Voice: "Yes God, I will change my ways, it's just..."

(God) " It's just what my Voice?"

Voice: "I just hate Kayden so much."

(God) "Yes I know my Voice and that hate is leading you straight to Hell. Take heed my Voice, if you fall too much, you will leave me with no choice but to send you to Hell where Kayden will be waiting for you to kick your ass forever."

The Book Of Hell (725.)

Angel – In the Hiding
Dressed-Like a Mortal
Come to My-Home
For-Some-Fine – Sinning

Bring-Me – What-I-Desire
Your-Body – Your-Book
The-Book of Hell – Which
I-Know – Is a Book of Lies

(Chorus)
The Book Of Hell
Was Created To Entice Me
Like I'm A Fool From Hell
The Book Of Hell
I Will Own – Just To Play The Game
That Heaven – Tries To Out Play Me

One-Angel – Not so Fresh – Anymore
Another – Angel – Laughing
Thinking-He – Won the Game
That-I – Manipulated
From-The-Very-Beginning

Angels – With-Tears of Rage
Knowing – They-Lost the Game
Kayden-Hart – Always-The-Winner
Until-I – Take-On-Heaven

(Chorus)
The Book Of Hell
Was Created To Entice Me
Like I'm A Fool From Hell
The Book Of Hell
I Will Own – Just To Play The Game
That Heaven – Tries To Out Play Me

Hell Is Not Bad (For A Man Like Me)

Not-Alone in Hell
That's-Where – I-Almost-Reign-Supreme
I'm-Given – Lots of Love
From-Lots of Fine – Evil-Ladies – &
Some-Fine – Demon-Ladies as Well

Hold-Me – Touch-Me – Never-Stop
Always-Repeated in My-Ears
I-Do-What-I-Want – With-Whomever-I-Want
I'm a Happy – Evil-Ruler of Hell
Whose-Name is Kayden-Hart

(Chorus)
Hell Is Not Bad
For A Man Like Me
Surrounded By All The Hot
Super – Evil – Sexiness
That A Ruler Of Hell
Like-Me – Needs And Wants

Not-Alone in Hell
That's-Where – I-Almost-Reign-Supreme
Millions and Millions of Souls
Belong to Me – For-Torturing
I-Tried to Kick-Back & Take-It-Easy

But-God – Would-Not-Let-Me
After a Few – Torturing of Evil-Souls
It-Became – No-Trouble at All
Ruling-Hell – With-Lots of Free-Time
To-Sex-It-Up & Slaughter-It-Out

(Chorus)
Hell Is Not Bad
For A Man Like Me
Surrounded By All The Hot
Super – Evil – Sexiness
That A Ruler Of Hell
Like-Me – Needs And Wants

www.ingramcontent.com/pod-product-compliance
Lightning Source LLC
Chambersburg PA
CBHW070510130626
46555CB00003B/1237